Also available in Large Print
by Janet Dailey:

The Rogue
Terms of Surrender
Touch the Wind
Western Man
Bluegrass King
Dangerous Masquerade
Fiesta San Antonio
For the Love of God
Foxfire Light
The Lancaster Men
Mistletoe and Holly
Night of the Cotillion
Night Way
The Second Time
Separate Cabins
Silver Wings, Santiago Blue
Wildcatter's Woman

Janet Dailey

DAKOTA DREAMIN'

G.K.HALL &CO.
Boston, Massachusetts
1986

Published in Large Print by arrangement
with Mills & Boon Limited.

G. K. Hall Large Print Book Series.

Set in 16pt Plantin.

Library of Congress Cataloging in Publication Data

Dailey, Janet.
  Dakota dreamin'.

  (G. K. Hall large print book series)
  1. Large type books.   I. Title.
[PS3554.A28D29   1986]   813'.54   85–16372
ISBN 0–8161–3894–X

DAKOTA DREAMIN'

All the characters in this book have no existence outside the imagination of the Author, and have no relation whatsoever to anyone bearing the same name or names. They are not even distantly inspired by any individual known or unknown to the Author, and all the incidents are pure invention.

CHAPTER ONE

Fingers of shock continued to send tingles down her spine as Edie Gibbs stared at the cheque in her hands. Her mind refused to assimilate the number of digits in the dollar figure. She lifted a hand to touch her fingertips to her temple and let them glide into her soft brown hair.

'I . . . I don't think I quite understand, Mr Wentworth.' At last she found her voice, husky though it was, to address the lawyer sitting in the wingbacked chair her late husband had always occupied. 'When you phoned and asked to discuss my . . . my financial condition, I thought—' A bewildered laugh escaped her throat. 'It took all of our savings to pay the funeral costs. Here I've been worrying how I was going to earn enough money to keep the house. I thought you were going to tell me about a monumental pile of debts. But this?' Her confused hazel eyes sought the attorney's face as she lifted the cheque in a questioning fashion. 'Is it real?'

'I assure you it's very real.' The gentleness in his expression said he was

1

pleased his news was good.

'But I didn't know Joe had any insurance.' Edie stared at the slip of paper that represented so much money. 'We talked about it a long time ago, but we couldn't squeeze the premium payments into our budget.' Which raised another question, and again her gaze lifted to the attorney in curious demand. 'Where did Joe get the money to pay them?'

'I was just coming to that.' He opened the briefcase sitting on his lap and took out a sheaf of papers.

'May I look at that, Mom?' Her daughter reached over to take the cheque from her numbed fingers. The action drew an abstract glance from Edie that touched the ponytailed girl seated on the couch, before her attention was claimed by the documents the attorney was handing her. She glanced through them, but the legal jargon was beyond her comprehension.

'What does all this mean?' Again her hazel eyes were darkened with confusion.

'I believe your late husband did a lot of tinkering in his workshop,' the lawyer began.

'That's an understatement!' Edie declared in a silent and rueful laugh. 'Joe

2

spent nearly every spare minute he had in his workshop. He'd come home from the garage, shower, eat, and disappear into the shed until it was bedtime.' There was nothing malicious or resentful in her statement. It had been too much a part of the accepted routine. 'He loved working there. That was his escape.'

'It was a profitable escape. In with those documents there are registrations of patents, some of which your late husband was able to sell to auto manufacturers in Detroit,' John Wentworth explained.

'Patents?' Edie was beginning to think she would never escape this whirl of confusion. None of this was making any sense. 'Joe didn't even have a high school diploma.' Something he had been very selfconscious about. Without it, he hadn't been able to obtain any other job except that of a garage mechanic, a trade at which he had excelled, but he hadn't found much pride in it. 'He tried. He took night courses at school whenever he could, but—' She let the sentence trail off unfinished to gaze at the documents she held.

'Whatever your late husband lacked in formal education, he more than made up for it in natural inventiveness,' the attorney

3

assured her. 'The royalties off these patents will provide you with a very comfortable income for a good many years, Mrs Gibbs. Also I have a national firm negotiating to purchase the rights on two more of his patents.'

This was more than she could take in. The silence from her daughter and stepson indicated that they, too, were finding these announcements difficult to comprehend.

'I don't understand.' She shook her head in bewilderment, the softly curling length of her brown hair barely brushing her shoulders. 'Why ... Why didn't Joe tell me ... tell us about these patents?'

'I really can't answer that,' John Wentworth sighed. 'I know he seemed very selfconscious about his inventions, as if they were a fluke. He was determined that no one should know about them.'

'And the money from these patents went to pay the premiums on the insurance policy?' Edie made the statement into a question, seeking a reconfirmation of his earlier explanation.

'The vast majority of it, yes,' the attorney nodded. 'He seemed determined that you would be taken care of in the event anything happened to him. It was almost as

4

if he had a premonition.' He removed another set of papers from his briefcase and handed them to Edie. 'This is a summary, and a projection of your annual income under the present agreements.'

He leaned forward to go over them with her. Edie listened and followed his moving finger down the list, but it was all a haze, something not quite real. She had been so braced for bad news that being presented with a pot of gold was something that seemed too good to be true.

Beneath her suntanned complexion, there was a white of shock. Features that were usually so animated with her irrepressible zest to meet life and its problems head-on were blank of expression. Her youthfully slim but mature figure was clad in the sombre colours of mourning, but she seemed too young to be a widow, the attorney thought—or to have a grown daughter, for that matter. Either way, this very attractive woman was not at all the way he had pictured Joseph Gibbs' wife, but it had been said that opposites attract. He noticed the stunned light in her large eyes.

'Let me make a suggestion, Mrs Gibbs,' he said. 'I'll leave these papers for you to look over, and you can call me in a couple of days. I'm certain you're going to have some questions, and it would be wise if we discussed the possibility of some financial investments for your future.'

'Yes, I would like a few days to think about it,' Edie agreed a little numbly, and belatedly started to rise.

'I'll walk Mr Wentworth to the door, Edie,' the young man seated on the couch volunteered.

'Thanks, Jerry—and I will call you, Mr Wentworth,' Edie added.

Her confusion began to sort itself as the front door was opened and closed, but she still felt stunned by the unexpected turn of events. At the sound of approaching footsteps, she lifted her gaze from the papers in her hand.

'Did you know about this, Jerry?' It was possible, since her stepson had often helped Joe in his workshop at weekends. Her gaze curiously searched his face, features steady and reliable like his father's. Except that his blue eyes often held the twinkle of humour, his mouth smiled easily, and his sandy brown hair was shaggy in a carelessly attractive way.

'I remember once he was trying to

modify one of the new emission control devices, but no—' he shook his head and paused by her chair to take the papers from her hand and leaf through them, '—I didn't know anything about patents.'

'You'd better take this cheque, Mom.' Alison shoved it into her hands. 'I can't believe we have so much money. Last night I couldn't sleep, worrying that I might have to sell one of my horses. Now—we could buy a whole stable full and not put a dent in that cheque.'

'I was afraid we were going to have to sell off the acreage,' Edie admitted. 'I know we've been able to board enough other horses to pay for the upkeep of our own, but the mortgage payment on this place, the utilities, groceries, all amounted to so much that—'

'You don't have to worry about that now, Edie,' her stepson voiced the very thought that was echoing through her mind.

'I know,' she murmured. 'But why didn't he tell us? Why didn't your father tell us?'

'Dad . . . was too easygoing,' Jerry said without criticising. 'You always were the battler in this family, Edie. You managed the money and kept the bill collectors at

7

bay during the hard times. Remember that time I got picked up for drinking on my sixteenth birthday; you were the one who went to bat for me with the judge.'

'But what has that got to do with this?' she argued. 'Think of how much money it cost him for this insurance policy. We could have used that money—or some of it. We could have taken a vacation, or bought a new car,' she added, remembering the clunker Joe had always coaxed into running.

'Just before I left for the Marines, Dad and I had a little talk—really one of the few we ever had. He told me that the one thing he had always regretted was marrying my mother when he was just sixteen. He not only had to quit school and get a job to support her, and later me, but he told me that he had to abandon his dreams.' Jerry sat down in the chair the attorney had vacated and leaned forward, clasping his hands together in a thoughtful attitude.

'That was one reason he was always so determined that the two of you had a chance at life.' Edie knew that story, and she was warmed by the memory of how profoundly her late husband had meant it. 'He told me that, too.'

'What he probably didn't tell you,' her stepson continued, 'was that he felt guilty for marrying you.'

'Guilty?' She was startled. 'Why?'

'After my mother died in that car accident, Dad didn't know how to cope with raising a kid on his own. Then he met you, Edie, and married you a week after you graduated from high school. He said he stole your dreams, too. Right away, you had a child to raise, debts to pay, a living to earn, and no time to be young and in love.'

'But Joe needed me. So did you,' Edie protested. 'I never felt that I missed anything.'

'It always bothered him that the two of you never had a honeymoon,' Jerry added.

'We had a honeymoon, a belated one,' she insisted. 'Don't you remember that camping trip we all took to the Black Hills?'

'What kind of honeymoon is that?' Alison laughed affectionately. 'You had two nosy kids along. It could hardly be classified as romantic by any stretch of the imagination!'

'Joe wasn't a very romantic person,' Edie admitted. It was the truth and she didn't feel she was being unkind to his memory to say so. His other qualities had more than

9

made up for his lack of sentimentality. Anyone who had ever known Joseph Gibbs had loved him, herself included. Honesty about his faults wouldn't diminish what he had been.

'To answer your question that started all this discussion,' Jerry inserted, 'I think Dad did what he did, and the way he did it, because he wanted you to be able to have your dreams, Edie, if anything ever happened to him.'

The telephone rang and Alison bolted from the couch. 'I'll get it!' As she raced to answer it, she ignored the extension in the living room in favour of the privacy offered by the kitchen phone. 'It might be Craig,' the quick explanation was tossed over her shoulder.

Edie watched the slim, long-legged girl sprint from the room. 'She hasn't heard from Craig since the funeral,' she commented to Jerry, referring to the boy Alison had been dating steadily since spring graduation, Craig Gurney.

'She won't either.' His face wore a very adult expression, revealing all of his twenty-four years of experience and more.

'Why?' Obviously her stepson knew something neither she nor Alison did.

'The word's out. Since Alison wouldn't deliver, Gurney is looking for a girl who will,' he said grimly. 'She's well rid of him, but I doubt if she'll agree. Don't tell her what I said. I don't think Alison realises how much guys talk.'

'I won't.'

'And let me know if Craig tries to see her again. I want to have a little talk with him if he does.'

It didn't take much reading between the lines to guess what Jerry would talk to him about. He had always been very protective towards Alison since the day Edie had brought her home from the hospital. The two shared a rare relationship for siblings. Rivalry between them was non-existent. Alison idolised her older half-brother and Jerry had long ago put his baby sister on a pedestal. Their closeness had always been a great source of pride and pleasure for Edie.

'Mom?' Alison stuck her head around the kitchen door. 'It's Mrs Van Doren.' She wrinkled her nose in dislike. 'She wants to know how soon you're going to have her sofa and chair re-upholstered. I explained about Dad's funeral and all. To hear her talk, you'd think Dad picked a terribly inconvenient time to die, the old

11

pruneface!'

Edie smothered a sigh of irritation, and tried to remember how much work was left on the items. 'Tell her I'll have them finished by Friday.'

'I'll tell her.' Alison disappeared behind the door.

Doing upholstering in her home had been one of the ways Edie had supplemented their income. Joe's salary had barely been able to stretch to meet their necessities. With the house, the garden, and taking care of the horses they boarded on the acreage, it hadn't been feasible for Edie to have a job in town. But she had discovered there were any number of things she could do at home to earn extra money.

'There's something I didn't make clear when we were talking a minute ago about the money Dad left you,' Jerry said. 'He left it for you, Edie, not for me or Alison. You're the only mother I've ever known. I may not call you that, but you are. I don't want you to think that we need any of that money—or should have any of it.'

'But—' she attempted a protest.

But Jerry interrupted, 'I mean it. You're only thirty-six, Edie. You're a very attractive woman with your whole life

12

ahead of you yet.'

'You're very good for my ego, Jerry,' Edie smiled, and would have continued, but he wouldn't let her.

'Dad wanted you to have it. I know I speak for Alison when I say that we want you to have it. We know how much you've sacrificed for us. How long has it been since you bought a new dress?' he challenged.

'How long has it been since I needed a new one?' she joked, because her husband hadn't been the type to socialise or go out for an evening, even if they could have afforded it. He preferred a home-cooked meal to any restaurant fare.

'With that money—' Jerry gestured towards the cheque in her hand, '—you can buy yourself a whole new wardrobe, travel, have fun, do anything you want.' As he was making the statement, Alison re-entered the living room in time to hear it.

'There's something else you can do, too, Mom,' she inserted, pausing to sit on the arm of Edie's chair. 'I was thinking about it in the kitchen after I hung up from talking to Mrs Van Doren. You could open up your own upholstery shop, go into business for yourself. Everybody around here knows how good you are at it.'

13

Owning her own business? Edie considered the idea, then dismissed it with a slight negative shake of her head. 'It would mean having a shop in town and spending most of the day inside when I'd rather be outdoors. No, I don't think I'd like that, in spite of the challenge. As for travelling, there are a lot of places I'd like to see, but—' She sighed, without finishing the statement, because she doubted if she would find much enjoyment in sightseeing alone. There would always be the memory of how much fun they had had as a family on that camping trip to the Black Hills of South Dakota and the instantaneous love she had felt for that Indian land.

'It isn't anything you have to decide now,' Jerry reminded her.

'No. And I don't intend to make any rash decisions about it either,' she smiled firmly.

'I would be surprised if you did, Edie,' Jerry declared, and pushed his lanky frame upright. 'It's just about chore time, so I'd better get back to the farm.' Since he had returned home after his tour of enlistment with the Marines, Jerry had worked for a large, corporately-owned farm with an enormous acreage of crops as well as a cattle feed-lot operation.

'I'm glad you could get time off from work to come over while the attorney was here,' said Edie.

'Yeah—well, it was too wet to be in the fields today anyhow, so—' He shrugged away the rest of the sentence.

'Speaking of chores,' Edie glanced at her daughter, 'we have some horses that need to be grained.'

'And stalls to be cleaned,' Alison grimaced. 'I'd better go and change.'

'Me, too,' Edie agreed, glancing down at her brown dress.

Jerry had started towards the front door. 'I'll probably be over Sunday, unless we start haying.'

'Sunday dinner will be at one o'clock, as always,' Edie told him before she followed Alison up the stairs to the bedrooms on the second floor.

After the front screen door had slammed shut, the engine of Jerry's pick-up roared to life in the yard of the old farmhouse. Edie paused at the open door of her daughter's bedroom. She watched for a silent second as Alison dragged a pair of worn blue jeans and an old shirt from her closet. It didn't seem possible that Alison would be eighteen in two short months.

15

'Did you want something, Mom?' Alison glanced up to see her standing in the doorway.

'I was just wondering—' she began, and changed to a more direct approach. 'Do you want to go to college, Alison?'

'I thought we'd been through all that.' Alison widened her brown eyes in mock exasperation.

'I know we talked about it before you graduated, but—' Edie paused, '—I want to be certain you refused because you didn't want to go and not because you knew we couldn't afford it. With the insurance money—'

'No, Mom,' Alison interrupted firmly. 'I don't want to go to college. I'm not college material—look at my grades. Besides, I'm like my dad. I don't have any ambition beyond having a nice home and family some day.'

'I don't think you're being exactly fair about your father,' Edie was immediately defensive, because she knew too well the night courses Joe had taken in an attempt to better himself.

'Yes, I am,' Alison insisted. 'I know why Dad never said anything about those inventions of his. He didn't want people to

16

treat him like someone he wasn't. He was just a mechanic, a good one, but just a mechanic. He wasn't ashamed of it, and neither am I.'

'That doesn't explain why he didn't tell us.' Edie returned to the question that kept nagging her.

'Don't you see, Mom? If he had told you, you'd have been so proud of him you would have told everybody. Can you imagine how someone like Mrs Van Doren would have started fawning over him, saying how clever he was. Dad couldn't have stood that. Dad just wasn't the type that ever wanted to be the centre of attention.'

'Yes, I suppose you're right,' Edie sighed, seeing the logic of her daughter's explanation.

In a town the size of this small Illinois community, Joe's inventions would have been big news. And Joe couldn't have coped with being a minor celebrity. Heavens, he hadn't even been able to cope with raising a small boy on his own, yet he had been such a strong, stalwart man in many ways.

'Look at me. I'm good with animals, breaking and training horses and such,' Alison continued, untying her wraparound skirt to toss it on the bed and tugging on her jeans. 'I know you once mentioned that I could become a vet, but all that anatomy stuff is beyond me. I can't even pronounce some of the diseases, let alone spell them. But, between the money I got from selling Fiesta's colt and what I'll be able to save working as a carhop at the drive-in this summer, I'll be able to pay for that horseshoeing course this fall. Then we won't have the expense of shoeing our horses, and I can make extra money by shoeing the horses we board.'

'One thing is certain—I don't think we'll ever be without horses,' Edie stated with a somewhat wry smile.

'Yeah,' Alison agreed, and looked up to reveal the impish twinkle in her brown eyes. 'We're both horse-crazy. Dad loved them, too,' she added, a faint sadness touching her smile, before it brightened. 'Even if we never could get him to climb on one.'

'Yes, that's true.'

'You'd better hurry up and get changed, Mom.' She leaned against the single bed to pull on her boots. 'I want to work Fiesta's filly at halter and I'll probably need your help at first.'

'I won't be a minute,' Edie promised, and moved away from the door to her own room.

It was funny how young Alison seemed to her, yet she had been a few months younger than her when she had married Joe straight out of high school. Edie walked to the closet to remove her old clothes. Now there were only her clothes in the closet; she had given all of Joe's to the church. Not that he'd had many, since he'd rarely worn anything but garage overalls. The greasy smell of them still lingered in the air. She wondered how long it would take before the smell faded.

While she dressed, her gaze strayed to the framed photographs on the dresser. One was a picture of the four of them taken ten years ago at Christmas, the most recent picture she had. Everyone · was smiling except Joe, whose face was in the shadow of the Christmas tree. The second and third frames held yellowed photographs of her parents and her two brothers, and her grandparents.

Their deaths, when Edie was only four, was a tragedy still talked about in the small Illinois community, almost an entire family, save Edie, wiped out in a single car

19

accident. She had been staying with her uncle, who subsequently took her in and raised her with his children. She had always been treated on an equal basis with her cousins, yet she had never felt that she truly belonged to their family unit.

In the spring of her senior year at high school, she had met Joe. At almost the same time her uncle had announced that they were moving to California where he had been transferred with a promotion. Edie hadn't wanted to go. And the more she saw of Joe and five-year-old Jerry, the more she realised how much they needed her—and how much she needed them.

All in all, she had had a good life, and a good marriage. She didn't regret it.

★   ★   ★

The next three months became an adjustment period for Edie, turning into a single woman again. Although she was used to making most of the decisions since Joe had so often been pre-occupied with his work or projects, there had always been the comforting knowledge that she could consult him when a problem arose. Now, virtually everything was solely her decision—from what time to get up to what to fix for dinner.

The one major decision she had postponed making—what to do with the money? She had discussed it with John Wentworth, the attorney. As soon as various friends and acquaintances learned about it, they volunteered suggestions. To this point, she had spent only a very tiny portion of it since she had continued to live on the strict budget they had had before. Nearly all of it was presently secured in an interest-bearing account, waiting for her decision.

One thing kept running through her mind whenever she thought about how she should use it. Jerry's comment that Joe had wanted her to have her dreams kept echoing back. At first she had dismissed the possibility because, on the surface, her dream seemed ludicrous and impractical. Although she never discussed it with anyone, not even Jerry or Alison, the idea kept coming back. Each time she found more and more reasons to make it seem plausible.

Finally she realised that she had to sound out her idea on Jerry and Alison. She needed their reaction to her proposal.

Without their support, she wouldn't be able to achieve her goal. The opportunity came on Sunday when Jerry arrived to have dinner with them.

Setting the platter of roast pork on the table, Edie sat in the chair opposite Jerry at the head of the table. She waited until Alison had offered the blessing and the food was being passed around.

'Mmm, you outdid yourself today, Edie,' Jerry declared, inhaling deeply the fragrant aroma of the sage dressing accompanying the pork. 'After a week of eating what comes out of the tin cans Chuck opens, this is manna from heaven!'

'Is it true that Craig is going out with Chuck's sister?' Alison demanded.

Jerry measured his half-sister with a sidelong glance, then nodded, 'Yes, it's true,' and helped himself to a heaping mound of mashed potatoes.

'I thought so.' It was a somewhat choked response that Alison tried to hide.

'I was cleaning a closet this week and ran across a couple of boxes pushed way to the back. You'll never guess what I found in one of them,' Edie stated, and didn't make them ask. 'Old snapshots of our trip to the Black Hills. They're on the buffet table

22

behind you, Alison.'

The distraction was one her daughter sought, and she reached back to remove the packet of photographs from the bureau top. 'That old Brownie camera took good pictures, didn't it?' she remarked after she had glanced through the first couple of snapshots. 'How old were we, Mom? Oh, Jerry, look at this one!' she laughed, and instantly handed it to him.

'I think you were eight and Jerry was fourteen,' Eddie replied.

'You were a beanpole then,' Alison teased her brother.

'You were pretty skinny yourself,' he retorted goodnaturedly.

'Look! This is really a terrific picture of the Four Faces at Mount Rushmore!' Alison handed him another. 'Here's one of the buffalo herd!' As she continued to pass the snapshots on to him, Jerry would sneak a bit of food and lay his knife and fork down in time to take the next one she handed him. 'We had so much fun on that trip,' she sighed.

'Do you remember this, Edie?' Jerry handed her one of the pictures, a laughing gleam in his eyes. 'You were trying to cook hamburgers on an outdoor grate. They kept

23

breaking in half and falling through on to the coals.'

'And Joe kept rescuing them,' Edie remembered.

'They were the grittiest hamburgers I've ever eaten,' he concluded.

'Definitely not one of my more memorable meals,' she agreed with a laugh.

'Would you just look at that country? Isn't it beautiful?' Alison sighed, and handed Jerry a photograph taken of the wild, rolling landscape. 'Do you remember how we all started dreaming about owning a ranch there some day? Even Dad?'

'Do I remember!' Jerry laughed shortly. 'We planned how many acres we were going to have, how many head of cattle it would hold, how much hayground we'd need for winter feed, how many horses we should have. Dad and I were even going to trap in the winter so Edie could have a fur coat.'

'You called it our Dakota dream ranch, didn't you, Mom?' Alison remembered with a faraway look.

'It doesn't have to be just a dream ranch,' Edie said carefully. 'We could have it now.'

Alison stared at her for a long moment. 'We could, couldn't we?' she breathed in realisation.

Edie turned her gaze to the young man seated across from her. Astonishment was written in his features. He set his fork down again, the food on his plate forgotten, as he searched her face.

'You're serious about this, aren't you?' His response was almost an accusation.

'Yes.' She was holding her breath.

'Do you know how much a ranch out there would cost?' Jerry questioned on a note of disbelief.

'I have a pretty good idea,' Edie nodded.

'We can afford it.' Alison was giving the idea her full support.

'Even after the down-payment, there would be enough money left out of the insurance to buy some stock and have a year's working capital.' She had already done some rough figuring in her head. 'There would still be some money coming in from the patents besides that.'

Jerry obviously found it difficult to argue with that. He shook his head and glanced at the photographs scattered across the table amidst the bowls of food. 'I suppose finding these pictures made you think about it.'

'No. I went looking for them, because I remembered what you said about Joe

25

wanting me to use the money to fulfil my dreams,' she explained. 'Except this isn't just my dream. It was *our* dream—yours, Alison's, Joe's, and mine.'

'I think it's the greatest idea I've ever heard,' Alison enthused.

'All right.' Jerry was still thinking, mulling it all over. It was what Edie wanted him to do. 'You can afford it, and it's something you've wanted. But how on earth are you going to run it? What do you know about running a ranch?'

'Most of it's common sense,' Edie reasoned. 'And I'm not completely without experience, limited though it is. I was raised on my uncle's farm. I've hayed, drove tractors, doctored sick animals, and a hundred other things. I've certainly had a lot of experience mending fences and I've been riding horses since I was five. None of that means I can handle the operation of a ranch by myself.'

'I'm relieved to hear you admit that.' Jerry leaned back in his chair, a vaguely mocking smile curving his mouth.

'However,' Edie paused for effect, 'I think I might know where I can get some qualified help to work with me.' She glanced at her daughter. 'There's you, for

26

instance, Alison. Now that you and Craig are finally through, you might consider coming with me. Between the two of us, we've delivered our share of foals, including the breech birth Fiesta had this last time. Cows can't be that much different. Besides, you've enrolled in that horseshoeing course, a skill that will definitely come in handy on a ranch.'

'I'll pack tomorrow, Mom,' Alison promised.

'What about you, Jerry?' Edie glanced at her stepson, who was the big question mark in her mind. 'You're the one with the experience. You've worked practically every summer on the farm with that feed-lot information. You have all the first-hand knowledge about cattle. Is there someone special here you wouldn't want to leave?' Since he had moved out she knew very little about his social life, except that he dated, but she didn't know of any girl he was dating steadily.

'No, there's no one special,' he admitted, and Edie could see he was weakening.

'There is one thing I would want clear from the very start,' she said. 'This is going to be a family ranch, especially if we're all working for it. We'll all have an interest in

27

it and, let's hope, a share of the profits. Thanks to your father, I don't *have* to do anything. It's what I want and what I think is fair. The two of you are going to work just as hard as I am to make the ranch successful. What's your answer, Jerry? Do you think you'd like to go into partnership with me and Alison?' she challenged.

He shook his head and smiled crookedly. 'It's so insane it just might work, do you know that?'

'That's what I thought!' Edie laughed, unable to check the flow of happiness at his silent agreement.

'We're really going to own a ranch!' Alison said it aloud as if she needed it repeated to believe it.

'We have an awful lot to do,' Edie sobered. 'First we're going to have to get in touch with a real estate company to find out what's on the market. We're all agreed on South Dakota, aren't we?'

'How else are we going to have a Dakota dream ranch?' Jerry mocked.

'And we aren't going to jump on the first place that's for sale, either,' she insisted. 'We aren't in any hurry, so let's find the right ranch for us, agreed?' Both nodded.

'What about this place?' Jerry wondered.

28

'We'll sell it,' Edie decided. 'Burn our bridges. Of course, that means the house and barn are going to need a fresh coat of paint. The fences, too.'

'We'd better wait to put it up for sale until we're fairly sure we've found a ranch,' Jerry cautioned.

'Yes, otherwise we'll have to find a place to keep our horses until we move,' Alison agreed, then asked, 'We are taking our horses, aren't we?'

'Definitely,' Jerry nodded, and glanced questioningly at his half-sister. 'Didn't you say that buckskin you bought last winter would make a good roping horse?'

'I think so. Try him out this afternoon and see for yourself,' she suggested.

'I'll do that.'

Alison rose from her chair. 'I'm going to get a paper and pencil so we can make a list of all the things we need to do. This is going to take some organisation!'

CHAPTER TWO

Needless to say, the Gibbs family decision was scoffed at, ridiculed, and the butt of many jokes in the area. No one quite believed they really intended to go through with it.

It wasn't easy to carry out their plan either. To begin with, there weren't many ranches for sale in the Black Hills region of South Dakota. Those that were, they were forced to reject as too costly, too large, or too small. But Edie persisted in trying, and with her as their leader, Jerry and Alison followed suit.

The waiting time was not idly spent. The quarter horses Alison had trained for the show ring and speed events became one of their joint projects, retraining them for working use. Two of the five horses had to be sold when they proved too nervous and unsuitable. In addition, Alison completed her horseshoeing course, while Edie and Jerry read every available piece of literature, pamphlets and books regarding ranch management, cattle, and land use. Others didn't take their plans seriously, but they did.

Four months from the Sunday they had sat around the table, made their decision, and begun their plans, the real estate agent called to tell Edie about a ranch that had just been placed on the market.

30

The owner, an elderly man, was being forced into retirement by an injury. Everything about the ranch sounded ideal, from its total acreage, the amount of pasture land and hayground, ample water supply, to the financial terms of the sale. Leaving Alison behind to look after the horses and the house, Edie and Jerry flew to Rapid City for a first-hand look at the ranch to be certain it was what had been represented to them.

The real estate agent met them at the airport and drove them out to the property. Snow covered the land, hiding more than it revealed as it followed the curvature of the hills and dipped into gullies. The dark green of pines was scattered across the winterscape. Driving into the ranchyard, Edie viewed the outbuildings with their snow-covered roofs and drifts banked close to their walls. There was no movement, no sign of stock, but smoke curled out of the chimney of the house to wind a white trail against a startling blue sky.

'The buildings look run down, don't they?' Jerry observed in a remark to Edie.

'Let's hope their appearance is deceiving,' she replied equally low. 'They must be structurally sound or they would have collapsed.'

The <u>tyres</u> crunched in the snow as the real estate agent slowed the car to a stop in the centre of the yard. Switching off the engine, he glanced at them. 'Would you like to walk around outside first? Anson Carver, the owner, is on crutches, so we'll have to show ourselves around. The footing is too tricky for him to be hobbling about on.'

'We'll look around first,' Edie agreed with his suggestion.

She buttoned the top buttons of her fleece-lined suede parka as Jerry stepped out of the car and pulled his cowboy hat low on his forehead. Edie discovered why when she slid out and a stiff wind blew its icy breath over any exposed skin. Bareheaded, she turned up the fleece collar of her coat and buried her hands in the warm pockets.

They tramped around and through the ranch buildings. As Edie had suspected, the barns and sheds appeared soundly built. There were boards that needed replacing, some window panes were broken, and the sliding track for the barn door had broken and another side door was precariously hinged. The signs of repair they did see were the 'lick-and-a-promise'

32

kind. Even the corral and holding pens of the ranchyard were constructed out of an assortment of materials, boards, wooden posts, split rails, whatever was handy and the right length at the time.

Trying to hold the front of his topcoat shut against a tugging wind, the agent produced an aerial photograph of the property and orientated them to their location so he could point out boundaries and landmarks. The picture had been taken during the summer, so it was difficult to recognise much when the wild and rolling terrain was blanketed with snow.

They wandered farther out from the ranchyard into the near pasture. The snow was nearly to the top of Edie's insulated boots, a thin crust on the top that crunched with each step. Jerry paused to sweep away a patch of snow with his boot. Beneath the snow was a tangle of long yellow grass, frozen together in thick clumps. The agent was busy extolling the merits of the place, stressing its wild, natural beauty. It took a few pointed questions from Edie regarding more practical matters like how many head of cattle they could expect the land to support before he realised she would not be swayed into buying a place because of its beauty.

When they turned back towards the ranchyard, Edie moved to the fence row where a strip had been drifted clear of snow parallel to the line. Her foot slipped on a patch of ice and she grabbed for a post to keep from falling into a drift. Instead of supporting her, the wooden post gave under the pressure of her grasping hand, and only Jerry's quick reflexes kept her from stumbling to her knees.

'It must have rotted through at the base,' he muttered grimly under his breath, and ran a calculating eye along the fence line.

Edie knew what he was thinking. The entire property would probably need new fencing. 'This place needs a lot of work.'

'You can say that again,' Jerry agreed before they caught up with the agent.

The house was in no better repair than the rest of the buildings. It was a one-storey, rambling affair that appeared to have had rooms added on with no attempt to adhere to design. White paint was chipped and peeling away to expose grey boards. A knock on the door brought a summons to enter. The interior of the house was as cheerless and dingy as the outside. After the brilliance of the outdoors with the bright sun glaring off white snow, it took Edie a moment to adjust to the gloom.

The front door had opened directly into a living room where an old wood stove was giving off waves of heat. The sudden change in temperature made Edie's chilled skin tingle with needle-sharp pain. The cold had nipped her cheeks red and made her facial muscles stiff, while the wind had tousled her hair into casual disorder. She paused inside the door to unbutton her coat and smooth her hair, not wanting to track into the house with her snow-wet boots on. The real estate agent didn't appear to suffer from any such compunction and walked to a corner of the room where an old man sat in an armchair with one plaster cast leg propped on a footstool.

'Hello, Mr Carver. I'm Ned Jenkins from the real estate office,' the agent introduced himself. 'I telephoned you this morning to let you know I was bringing these people out to look at your ranch.'

'I remember,' a gruff voice answered, then the old man turned his keenly piercing gaze to the pair standing by the door. He waved an impatient hand for them to enter the living room. 'Come in. I don't intend to shout across the room to carry on a conversation with you.'

'Let me take off my boots first so I don't track,' said Edie, and bent to unfasten them. A puddle of dirty water was already beginning to form on the floor around her feet.

'Take them off if you've a mind to,' the old man scoffed, 'but a little water and mud ain't going to be strange to this floor.'

Regardless of his lack of concern, Edie went ahead and removed her boots, and Jerry did likewise. She set them neatly against the wall before crossing the room in her stocking-clad feet to meet the present owner.

Aware that Jerry was a step behind her, she stopped in front of the old man's chair. Age had wrinkled his sun-browned face and thinned his hair until there were only wispy grey tufts on top of his head with no attempt to tame them in place.

The real estate agent introduced them. 'Mr Carver, this is Mrs Gibbs from Illinois. Mr Anson Carver, the owner of the property.'

'How do you do, Mr Carver.' Edie was faintly surprised by the firmness of the grip of the withered hand that clasped hers.

'This is her son, Jerry Gibbs,' the agent continued the introductions.

'How do you do, sir.' The crispness of Jerry's acknowledgment hinted at the years he had spent in the military.

'Your son?' Anson Carver's sharp gaze swung back to her, sweeping her from head to foot. 'What did you do? Have him straight out of puberty?'

At first Edie was taken back by the crude and blunt question, then a rueful smile slanted her mouth. 'Jerry is my stepson,' she admitted.

'Where's your husband? How come he sent you instead of coming himself?' he demanded with continuing bluntness.

'I lost my husband eight months ago, Mr Carver. I'm a widow,' Edie told him in a voice that invited no sympathy.

Again she was subject to his scrutiny as he took special note of her figure revealed by the unbuttoned parka swinging open. 'With a face and a body like yours, you won't be a widow for long.'

After his previous remarks, Edie wasn't shocked by this statement from him. 'I believe you're flattering me,' she smiled it away.

'At my age, I don't have to say things I

37

don't mean. In fact, I can say a lot of things I do mean.' His smile indicated that he derived tremendous pleasure from doing just that, and shocking people in the process. Definitely, an irascible rascal, Edie decided. 'Pull up a chair and sit down. I'm getting a crick in my neck looking up at you,' Anson Carver ordered.

The agent brought a straight chair over for Edie to sit on while Jerry got a chair for himself. It was too hot this close to the heating stove to leave her coat on, so Edie took it off and draped it on the chairback.

'So you came out here to look at my ranch,' the older man declared in a gruff challenge. 'What do you think of it?'

Edie took a breath, then told him. 'To be frank, Mr Carver, you've let it go to hell.'

Her candour startled him. With a frown, he grumbled, 'The place seemed to get too big for me to handle alone—either that or I got too old. I admit it needs fixing up here and there.'

'Here and there?' She lifted a challenging eyebrow. The heavily ribbed biscuit-coloured pullover she was wearing with her brown corduroy slacks gave her a very earthy and countryish look. 'Your buildings are in need of repair. I doubt if

38

there's a section of fence on the property that doesn't need to be replaced. And who knows what other things the snow is hiding? It's going to take a lot of labour and material to bring this place up to par.'

'In other words, you think I'm asking too much for the ranch?' he bristled.

'Yes, I do,' Edie admitted.

'I suppose your husband left you a bunch of money and you've decided to invest it in a cattle ranch.' He sounded faintly contemptuous, but Edie had faced that attitude many times in these months since they had made their decision. 'Who's gonna run it for you?'

'Nobody is going to run it for us. We're going to do it ourselves,' she said, nodding towards Jerry to include him in her plural pronoun.

'Do you think you can handle it?'

'We'll do a better job than you have lately,' Edie shrugged.

'You're pretty frisky for such a slip of a gal. If push come to shove, you'd do some shoving yourself, wouldn't you?' he grinned unexpectedly. 'What do you think this place is worth?'

Edie told him and added her terms. They haggled back and forth for several minutes.

Every time the real estate agent tried to make a relevant point, the old man told him to shut up. They went through a rapid series of compromises until the last difference in their two positions was settled.

'Lady, you drive a hard bargain, but you just bought yourself a ranch.' The man extended his hand to shake on the deal. He sliced a piercing look at the agent. 'Did you make a note of all the terms so we can draw up an agreement?'

'Yes, sir. I—'

'Fine. Start writing it up.' Anson Carver was quick to dismiss him from the conversation. Now he was directing his attention to Jerry. 'You look like you got a head on your shoulders, boy. Do you think you and your stepmomma can handle this place?'

'I do, or I wouldn't be here,' Jerry told him with a faint smile.

'Got any more like him?' Anson Carver shot the question at Edie.

'I have a daughter. She's looking after our place in Illinois while we're here.'

He rested his head against the chairback for a moment. 'I'm glad someone like you is buying the ranch. I didn't want to see it

40

gobbled up into somebody else's holdings,' he explained rather absently. 'I've lived in this house seventy-two years. It's good to know that somebody will be living in it when I'm gone.'

'Where will you go, Mr Carver?' Edie asked.

He pursed his lips, puckering as if there was a bad taste in his mouth. 'I'm moving to my granddaughter's in Deadwood. She's got a room all fixed up for me, she says.'

'You'll always be welcome to stop by,' Edie told him.

His gaze swung to her, a sudden twinkle lighting his eyes with mischief. 'A widow and two kids,' he chortled in apparent delight. 'I'd love to see his face when he finds out!'

'Whose face?' A frown flickered across her forehead.

'It's a private joke.' He didn't explain. 'You won't understand until after you've lived here for a while. At my age, there are few pleasures left in life that I can enjoy. But to know that I'm the one to show the he-bull in these parts that he can't have everything the way he wants it gives me a lot of satisfaction. Mind you, it's nothing personal, but I'll have many a laugh over this in that room in Deadwood.'

'Does it have something to do with the ranch?' Edie persisted, puzzled by his answer and certain that he intended her to be.

'You aren't going to have any problems that you can't handle,' he assured her. 'When do you want possession?'

Edie glanced at Jerry. There were a great many things that had to be done in Illinois—put their house and acreage up for sale, and pack. And there was all the legal paperwork involved in buying this place.

'The end of March? What do you think?' she asked.

'That sounds good to me,' Jerry nodded. 'Spring will be breaking. That gives us a little over two months.'

'Would that suit you, Mr Carver?' she asked.

'Fine. Make a note of that, Jenkins,' he ordered. 'While he's writing all this down, why don't you go into the kitchen, Mrs Gibbs, and fix us some coffee? I would, but—' he thumped the plaster cast on his leg, '—I don't get around too good.' He pointed to a hallway behind him. 'It's that way.'

'I don't mind at all,' Edie agreed, and

42

rose from her chair.

As she left the room she heard Jerry ask, 'When we were walking around outside, I didn't see any sign of livestock. Don't you have any?'

'No. When I got laid up, I didn't have any way of looking after them. And I never could keep good help on the place. So I asked ... my neighbour to round up anything that moved and sell it.'

Edie couldn't help thinking it was comforting to know they would have the kind of neighbours who were willing to help out in time of need.

★　　　★　　　★

Everything seemed to fall into place after that. Within a month after they had listed their Illinois property for sale, they had a buyer. All the legal paperwork for both the sale of their property and the purchase of the ranch was completed in two months. The last week there was a string of farewell parties for them.

Edie was aware that many people thought she was being disrespectful to Joe's memory by selling the place where they had lived and moving away. But Joe had made this chance possible, and she was convinced it would be a greater injustice to him if she didn't take it.

Happy seemed an inadequate description of the way she felt. She was excited, eager, looking forward to this new life and its challenges. It seemed an adventure. She wanted to laugh aloud, for no reason at all. And since she was alone in the cab of the rented U-haul truck, she did.

A series of signs was tacked to the row of fence posts along the highway. Edie read them with quick glances and reached for the mike of the CB radio, temporarily mounted on the dash. It had been one of the going-away presents.

'Breaker one-nine. This is the Dakota Dreamer in the rocking chair. How about that Pony Girl up there at my front door?' She used the CB radio jargon to call Alison in the car ahead of the truck.

'You've got the Pony Girl. Come back,' Alison responded.

'Did you read those signs we just passed? Come back.'

'I must have missed them. What did they say this time?' her daughter asked.

'It said: "You are entering God's country. Don't drive through it like hell",'

Edie told her.

'Yeah, so ease back on the hammer, Pony Girl,' Jerry joined their radio conversation. 'Your back door has a load of dogmeat, in case you've forgotten. Slow it down.' He was bringing up the rear of their small caravan in his pick-up truck, pulling the horse trailer loaded with their horses and gear.

'My foot's got heavy, Leatherneck. I'm easing it back,' Alison replied.

'Hey, Pony Girl,' Jerry called her back, 'if you see a rest area, pull over. I want to check the horses.'

'That's a ten-four,' Alison agreed.

And the radio went silent for a while in Edie's cab, except for the chatter of some other CB'ers some distance away. Her gaze strayed to the rolling landscape of the South Dakota prairie. Its flat appearance was deceptive as its grassed sod undulated towards the horizon. Trees, mostly cottonwoods, clustered wherever there was water. There was a timeless quality about this open expanse of land, stretching endlessly into the beyond, that had a magic all its own. Patches of snow could be seen in shadowed ditches, an indication that winter hadn't released its grip on the land.

45

After travelling almost a full hour, Edie saw the dark mass looming on the horizon. Her mouth barely curved as she recognised it, her pulse quickening in a surge of excitement. Again she reached for the CB mike to share her discovery with Alison and Jerry.

'Breaker one-nine for that Pony Girl and Leatherneck. Do you see that on the horizon?' she asked.

'Where?' Alison came back. 'You mean that mass of clouds? I hope we aren't in for a storm.'

'Those aren't clouds,' Jerry corrected. 'That's the Black Hills. Now you know how they got their name.'

'There's some roadside tables just ahead. It looks like there's room for all of us to park,' Alison told them. Edie saw the turning indicator blinking on the car ahead of her, and flipped hers on.

When the rental van filled with their furniture and belongings was parked and the motor switched off, Edie grabbed for her parka and the thermos of coffee from the passenger seat. Alison was already standing by the roadside picnic table, stretching and arching muscles cramped from long hours of driving. Yesterday they had started out at daybreak and continued till dark, crossing Iowa into Nebraska. Now the Black Hills dominated the horizon, rising above the prairie, pine-covered slopes giving the deceptive impression of darkness and earning the landmark its name. Their ranch, their new home, was on the western edge of this sacred Indian land within the National Forest.

'We don't have far to go now,' Edie declared as she joined Alison by the picnic table. A cold wind tried to slide its icy fingers inside the collar of her jacket, but Edie fastened the top button to keep it out.

'Mmm, coffee!' Alison took one of the cups and held it while Edie filled it half full. 'I wish I could have gone with you guys to see the ranch.'

'Don't be expecting too much,' Edie cautioned. 'The place is run down and needs a lot of work to put it in shape.'

'I hope there's enough coffee there for me.' Jerry paused beside her, wearing an insulated vest over his plaid flannel shirt, but otherwise coatless. He rubbed his hands together to warm them as Edie poured him half a cup of coffee, too. 'The ranch may not look like much, but we

47

know for sure it isn't worthless,' he said, picking up the conversation where Edie had left off.

'What?' At first Edie didn't follow his meaning, then she remembered with a nod of her head. 'You mean that offer.'

'Yes.' He sipped at the hot coffee. 'We could have sold the place for a handsome profit even before we'd signed the final papers to buy it.'

'Maybe we should have,' Alison suggested.

'Where would we have gone?' Edie reasoned. 'Our place was already sold, so we had to move. Who knows how long it might have taken us to find another ranch so ideally suited. Can you imagine how much it would have cost if we'd had to pay to board our horses?'

'I suppose you're right,' her daughter conceded.

Edie knew why her daughter was having doubts. The answer was simple—Craig Gurney. He had managed to turn up at every farewell party given for them. It was to Alison's credit that she had treated him coolly in the beginning, but Craig's persistence had her weakening towards the end.

48

'Speaking of horses,' Jerry paused to drain the last of the coffee from his cup and hand it back to Edie, 'I'd better check on them.'

Edie watched him for a second, then turned, a light of anticipation glittering in her eyes. Tomorrow they would be riding the horses on their very own ranch, exploring the property. Her mouth opened to share the thought with Alison until she saw that wistful, faraway look in her daughter's eyes as she looked back at the road they had travelled.

'Are you sorry we left, Alison?' Edie asked gently.

It was a full second before Alison blinked and let her gaze refocus. 'I . . .' she began uncertainly, then finished with a sighing, 'No.'

Masking her relief, Edie offered, 'More coffee? There's only a little bit left in the thermos.'

Alison held out her cup in silent acceptance. 'Mom, were you a virgin when you married Dad?' she asked thoughtfully.

Craig Gurney had to be responsible for that question, Edie thought, and replied, 'Yes.'

'You didn't . . . anticipate your wedding

or anything like that, did you?' Alison persisted.

'No.' A smile twitched at the corners of Edie's mouth, hinting at a pair of dimples. 'But it isn't easy to "anticipate" anything when you have a five-year-old boy along as chaperone on all your dates!'

While taking a sip of coffee, Alison was overcome by a laugh. She choked and sputtered, and coughed out the laugh. 'I'm sorry,' her eyes were brimming with tears and shining with laughter. 'But for a second I was trying to visualise Dad sweeping you off your feet. And he just wasn't the type,' she declared in a voice that bubbled with her amusement. 'I can't see Dad ever tempting any woman into a sinful situation. Maybe a daughter can't visualise her father as a lover.'

'Probably not,' Edie agreed, smiling with her daughter, knowing Alison wasn't criticising Joe.

'Dad was good-looking, in his own way,' Alison recalled, 'but he was never an exciting kind of man. I don't mean he was dull. I used to get so exasperated with him when he'd forget your birthday that I wanted to bat him over the head. One time I told him that instead of kissing you on the

50

cheek when he came home, he should take you in his arms and do it properly. Of course, he didn't take my advice,' she sighed in a gentle way to indicate it hadn't mattered.

'Joe wasn't very demonstrative, but he was a good man, the best.' There was a tiny catch in Edie's voice. While he hadn't been a passionate man, he had made her feel good—needed, wanted and loved.

'You miss him, too, don't you, Mom?' Alison offered in commiseration.

'Yes. It isn't so bad during the day, because he was usually at work. In the evenings, he was usually in his workshop. But when I wake up in the night and he isn't there to cuddle up to, that's when I really miss him,' Edie admitted softly, staring into her empty cup.

'Do you think you'll get married again, Mom?'

The question jerked Edie's chin up. After a startled second had passed, she emitted an incredulous and breathless laugh. 'Your father hasn't even been dead a year! I'm certainly not looking for a replacement.'

'But if you meet someone,' Alison persisted.

51

'If I met a man I thought I could love and who could love me, I would consider it.' What else could she say? She certainly wasn't going to pretend she was blind to the possibility that it might happen. Her life certainly wasn't going to come to an end if it didn't.

'They say that every man makes love differently, that just because you've been to bed with one man it doesn't mean the feeling will be the same with the next. It has to do with the two chemistries involved, I guess,' Alison volunteered the information absently.

'*They* say that, do they?' Edie mocked, amused by the 'voice of experience' talking. 'I'm afraid I wouldn't know about that.'

'Oh, Mom!' Alison blushed and laughed.

Edie joined in. 'I hope you don't object if I don't bother to check *their* theory to see if it's true or not.'

'I'll disown you if you do,' Alison continued to laugh.

'Hey! Come on, you two!' Jerry shouted from his truck. 'Let's get on the road. We still have a way to go and a lot of unloading to do before nightfall.'

'We'll be right there!' Alison called back, and handed the plastic coffee cup to Edie. 'I

52

think he's trying to tell us to hurry up,' she grinned.

'You could be right.' Edie stacked the cups inside one another and screwed them on to the thermos.

Jerry was in his truck with the motor running by the time Edie crawled into the cab of the rental van. She warmed up the engine and waited until Alison had pulled on to the highway before falling in behind the car. Jerry was right: they did have a way to go, and the last stretch would be on gravelled roads.

CHAPTER THREE

Stopped in the ranchyard, the three of them were slow to step out of their individual vehicles. When they did, they gravitated towards each other, unconsciously solidifying into a united front.

'It looks worse, doesn't it?' Edie remarked.

Without the pristine whiteness of snow-cover, the run-down condition of the ranch stood out against its stark background of brown grass and craggy hills with shaggy clusters of pines. The buildings were weathered and grey, the patchwork repairs telling their own tales of shoddy workmanship. The corral behind the barn looked incapable of holding a newborn calf. The house had four different colours of shingles on its roof.

'This is it?' Alison's sceptical expression revealed her opinion.

'I warned you it needed work,' Edie reminded her.

'I thought you meant a facelift, not major surgery,' she replied with faint disgust.

'The first thing that *has* to be done is fix that corral so we have somewhere to unload the horses,' Jerry stated with his usual practicality.

Glancing at the sun dipping towards the western horizon, Edie added, 'We'd better all help if we want it done before dark.'

They had practically rebuilt the corral before they were finished, replacing this post, bracing another, ripping out rotting boards and tearing barn stalls apart for replacement boards. When they were finished, it was almost twilight. The end result didn't look any more attractive than the previous corral, but they knew it was sturdy.

With the setting sun, the temperature was dropping. Although the hard labour had all three of them perspiring, Edie felt the clammy chill setting in. Jerry was manoeuvring the horse trailer into position to unload, with instructions from Alison. Edie glanced towards the bleak exterior of the house and the soot-blackened chimney on its roof.

'You two unload the horses. I'll see what I can do about getting a fire started in the house,' she said, and received an acknowledging wave from Jerry.

Without the clutter of Anson Carver's worn furniture, the interior of the house was more depressing than the exterior; the cold, dreary emptiness of the rooms not welcoming. To make matters worse, when Edie flipped the light switch to chase away the gathering shadows, nothing happened. It was the same with every light switch in the house, which meant they had no electricity. Evidently the power company had not carried out their instructions.

Sighing, Edie walked back outside to the rental van for the battery-operated flashlight. Somewhere, packed neatly away in boxes, there were candles and a hurricane lamp, but with her luck, Edie was positive it would be the last box.

The beam of the flashlight gave off enough illumination for her to check the wood stove to be certain the damper was open before she lit it. When the fire was blazing strongly, she left the living room to check out the rest of the house. What she found made her spirits droop even lower and remind her of Anson Carver's comment that his house had known dirt intimately. Cobwebs, dust, and dirt coated everything. And this was her new beginning on her dream ranch! Her mouth twisted in irony.

The front door was opened and she heard two pairs of footsteps stomp wearily into the house. 'I'm starving,' Alison mumbled. The comment was followed immediately by, 'Mom? What's the matter with the lights?'

She stepped into the hallway to flash the beam towards them. 'We don't have any electricity. There must have been a mix-up.'

'Oh, good grief!' her daughter exclaimed in disgust. 'Now we'll have to stumble around in the dark to unload everything. What about something to eat?'

'We'll probably have to settle for cold sandwiches,' Edie admitted in a sigh.

56

'Do you want me to bring in the ice chest and groceries from the truck?' Jerry asked.

'Yes—and all the cleaning supplies, too,' she added.

As Alison walked down the hallway illuminated by the flashlight beam, she ran into a cobweb. 'Ugh!' She wiped it off her face with an expressive grimace ᴄ distaste. 'This place is filthy!'

'Yes,' Edie agreed. 'I'm afraid all we're going to accomplish tonight is scrubbing out the bedrooms so we'll have a place to sleep.'

It was nearly midnight before all three bedrooms were cleaned, the bedroom furniture unloaded from the van, and the beds made. Alison unearthed the candles and kerosene lantern, which helped. They not only were without electricity, but also without hot water. None of them relished a cold shower, no matter how dirty they were, so Edie warmed a pail of water on the wood stove. They washed the worst of the dirt off and tumbled into their beds too exhausted to care.

The next morning they unloaded the rest of the furniture from the van. Edie left Alison and Jerry at the ranch to finish cleaning the house and arrange their belongings while she drove the rented truck into town to return it and find out what the problem was with the electricity. She expected to be finished by noon, and made arrangements with Jerry to pick her up at the grocery store.

It was almost three o'clock before she met him. What groceries they had needed, he had already bought and stacked in the front seat of the cab.

'I was beginning to wonder what had happened to you.' Jerry took one look at her seething expression and tried to hide a grin. 'I don't think I'll ask what kept you.'

'I've been getting the royal run-around,' she snapped, and crawled into the cab of his truck, pushing the grocery sacks out of her way, still fuming. 'I kept getting shoved from one person at the power company to another. First they tried to tell me that we hadn't requested service.'

'Did you show them a copy of the letter we sent?' Jerry started the motor and reversed away from the kerb into the street.

'Yes.' Edie glared out of the window at the boardwalks shaded by jutting overhangs of Western-styled buildings. 'Then they tried to tell me we hadn't made a deposit. I've never been any place where people were so incredibly ignorant and unco-operative!'

'Did you get it straightened out?'

'Finally. We're supposed to have the electricity connected late this afternoon.' She leaned back in her seat, rubbing her forehead where it was pounding.

'Should we hold our breath?' Jerry teased.

'They'd better have it turned on. I want a shower tonight.' She closed her eyes and tried to will away the angry tension. 'How's everything going at the ranch?'

'Okay. I left Alison cleaning the kitchen . . . and swearing,' he answered.

Edie opened one eye to look at him, an impish light dancing in the hazel depths. 'I hope she has it finished before we get back so we don't have to help.'

'Right!' Jerry tipped his head back to laugh a hearty agreement. 'My hands are starting to look all funny and pink from all that detergent water.'

Edie closed her eyes again and let the rhythm of the rolling wheels on the pavement soothe her into relaxing. When Jerry made the turn on to the gravelled road, she opened them to study the scenery racing by the pick-up window. Tall

59

ponderosa pines hugged the edges of the road to form a green corridor. Here and there, they thinned out to make a meadow of yellow grass. The winding gravel road alternated between sun and shadow. Beyond the pine branches there were glimpses of high mountains, granite rock interlacing with trees. A valley opened up, grassy and serene.

'Even with all the unexpected problems, I'm glad we're here,' Edie decided.

'So am I. None of us thought it was going to be easy. But we know all about work,' Jerry slid her a smile. 'We never have been afraid of it, and we have more reason than ever not to be now.'

'That's true,' she laughed softly. They had a ranch to build, and a future.

'Tomorrow we'll have to ride the perimeters, and check the fences.'

For the rest of the drive, they talked of the things that needed to be done in preparation for the stock cattle they intended to buy, as well as some yearling calves for fall sale. When they arrived at the ranch, Alison met them at the door, demanding to know where they had been. Edie and Jerry exchanged a silent look of humour. They knew Alison was disgruntled because she had been left to finish the cleaning alone, and they knew how much she detested housework. As Edie was relating her tale of battle with the power company, the lights came on, and Alison forgot her ill-temper to join in the cheers for Edie's triumph over the utility's red tape foul-up.

With the house in some semblance of order and as sparkling clean as the dingy place could ever be, the three went out to briefly exercise the horses, then brushed them down, and grained them for the night. At six-thirty, they sat down for the first home-cooked meal any of them had had in three days.

'Did you hear a car door slam?' Alison asked, and cocked her head to listen before helping herself to a second portion of macaroni and cheese.

'If you turned that radio down a notch, we might be able to hear ourselves think,' Jerry suggested dryly.

'It isn't that loud,' she protested, but reached behind her to turn down the volume of the radio on the kitchen counter.

Instantly there was a loud knock at the front door. Edie frowned in surprise and started to get up. 'Who could that be?'

61

'I'll answer it,' Jerry waved her into her seat. 'It's probably that real estate agent checking to see how we've settled in. Wasn't his name Jenkins?'

'I think so,' Edie agreed as he left the room. The lights flickered overhead and her mouth thinned into an angry line. 'Or maybe it's somebody with the utility company. I'd better go to the door, too.'

She emerged from the kitchen as Jerry opened the front door. Edie could tell by the reserved tone of his greeting that her stepson didn't know the person calling.

A pleasantly deep male voice responded, 'Good evening. I would like to speak with Mrs Gibbs if she's free.'

There was an impersonal quality to the request, yet it carried the crispness of authority. Edie noticed the way Jerry unconsciously squared his shoulders and stood a little straighter, as if facing a commanding officer.

'If you'll step inside, I'll call her.' Jerry swung the door wide to admit the man. As he pivoted, he saw her in the hall. 'Edie, there's a man here to see you.'

Curious, she moved forward. The man was tall, over six feet. She knew that because he had to remove his hat and duck

62

his head to walk through the front door. He was wearing a tailored leather jacket that emphasised the width and breadth of his shoulders and the relative slimness of his hips. Western-cut brown trousers flared slightly over his boots.

Her first impression of the stranger reminded her of a range bull, all leashed power and raw virility. It was repeated in the way he carried himself with an aloof nobility. He held dominion over his kind, and it showed. Members of this proud, rugged breed were dangerous when riled, and implacable in the face of danger. Even the most powerful predators would veer away from this range bull.

And Edie found herself treading warily in his presence. When her gaze skimmed his hard-hewed features, there was nothing in the thrusting power of his jaw and chin, the slightly crooked bend of his nose, or the firmly cut line of his mouth to change her initial impression. The flecks of iron in his shaggy dark brown hair were a sign of maturity, a man in his prime, not an encroaching weakness. Or maybe her opinion had been influenced by the hardness of the iron-grey eyes taking note of her approach.

Her smile was pleasant enough when she stopped in front of him. It was only natural, Edie supposed, to feel intimidated by his size. She also understood why Jerry had felt the impulse to snap to attention, but she suppressed it. Here, she was the one in charge. The fact remained that, although this stranger was standing in her living room with his hat in his hand, there was nothing humble about him.

'I'm Edie Gibbs,' she confirmed her identity. 'You wanted to see me?'

The mocking glint that flashed in his eyes gave her the impression that he was mentally quirking an eyebrow at the information, although there wasn't a flicker of any such movement. His gaze started at the top of her head and slowly worked its way down.

First, Edie realised that she hadn't combed her hair since coming in the house from exercising and caring for the horses. Her golden-brown hair was undoubtedly windblown and tousled. His inspection of her face made her conscious that she wore no make-up, even her lipstick had been eaten off at the supper table. It took every ounce of willpower not to moisten her lips when he studied their contours.

His silent appraisal continued its downward progress, drawing her attention to the boy's flannel shirt she wore, a size too small. In consequence, the plaid material was stretched tautly across the rounded fullness of her breasts, the buttoned front gaping slightly. It wasn't a stripping look. A man like this knew what was underneath without needing to mentally disrobe a woman to get his kicks. Edie didn't know how she knew that, but she did. Yet it didn't make her feel any less uncomfortable.

Then his gaze was skimming her faded denims, hugging tightly to her slim hips and shapely thighs before running stovepipe-straight to her boots. He even took note of the scuffed and weathered leather of her boots, permanently stained with mud and manure.

When his metallic smooth gaze returned to her face, the tour of inspection hadn't taken more than twenty seconds, but it had seemed an eternity of irritated discomfort to Edie. The words burned on the tip of her tongue to tell him that she hadn't been expecting visitors—and he should have expected to find her still in work clothes from doing ranch chores, but she held them back, because she wasn't about to defend the way she dressed in her own home—not to a complete stranger.

'*You* are the widow Gibbs?' The inflection in the husky timbre of his voice smoothly demanded verification.

It had been an exasperating day. Irritation again raced through nerve ends that had only just begun to recover. His implication that she didn't fit the image of a middle-aged widow set her teeth on edge. Admittedly she was on the wrong side of thirty, but it didn't mean she had to be dumpy and plain or clad in black with smelling salts at hand.

'Yes, I am.' The faint note of belligerence in her answer didn't appear to register in his expression. She lifted her chin to an angle of controlled challenge as her smile lost its warmth. 'You have the advantage. You know who I am, but I don't know who you are.'

'Will Maddock.' He didn't extend his hand in greeting. 'I own the Diamond D Ranch.'

Edie guessed she was supposed to be impressed, but since she had never heard of it—or him—she simply filed the information away in her mind.

66

'The Diamond D?' Jerry spoke up. He had been standing to one side. 'I saw that brand on some cattle on my way into town this noon. They were in a pasture next to our property.'

At the sound of Jerry's voice, Will Maddock had turned his head to subject her stepson to his appraisal. He measured Jerry with a practised eye, noting his lanky but solidly muscled frame and the shadow of a man's beard on his cheek, not the peach fuzz of a boy.

'You own the land next to ours?' Jerry questioned.

'Yes.' It was a simple, straightforward answer.

'Then you're our neighbour,' Edie realised.

The iron-hard gaze swung lazily back to her. 'Yes.'

She stifled the resentment that she had begun to form against him. Will Maddock was obviously calling to welcome them to the area, a gesture of polite friendliness that shouldn't be slapped away simply because she had had a bad day and was therefore quicker to take exception. Possibly Will Maddock was the same neighbour who had rounded up and sold Anson Carver's

67

livestock when he was laid up. He struck her as the kind of man who you would want on your side if you were in trouble. She definitely wouldn't want him as an enemy.

'It's a pleasure to meet you, Mr Maddock.' She extended her hand in belated greeting.

He glanced at it, hesitated, then accepted the gesture. When his work-roughened hand closed around hers, Edie experienced a tremor of surprise. She had always thought Joe's hands were large, but her hand looked like a child's against Will Maddock's. It was such a strong, capable hand, it didn't need to assert its strength by crushing her fingers. There was the firm warmth of its clasp, then her hand was released. A little overwhelmed by the discovery, Edie didn't notice that Will Maddock hadn't returned her phrase, nor one like it.

Instead she turned to introduce Jerry and caught sight of Alison, who had slipped unnoticed into the room. 'This is my stepson, Jerry Gibbs, and my daughter Alison. Mr Will Maddock.'

Jerry stepped forward to shake hands with him, but Alison simply smiled and nodded from across the room. It was part of her natural reserve when meeting strangers, but not caused by shyness.

Remembering her manners, Edie invited, 'Won't you sit down, Mr Maddock? Let me take your coat.'

He accepted the invitation to have a seat, but refused the second suggestion, 'No, I won't be staying long.'

He did unbutton the leather jacket to let it swing open before sitting in the armchair that had always been Joe's favourite. But Edie never remembered Joe ever filling it the way this man did. In fact, it took on the appearance of a throne. Again there was that little flicker of resentment that Edie had to suppress.

'We'd just finished supper and were about to have some coffee when you arrived.' She told the white lie out of a sense of courtesy. 'Would you like a cup?'

'No.' His iron-flat gaze made a pointed glance towards Jerry and Alison. 'I would like to speak to you in private, if I may.'

The skin along the back of her neck prickled, irritated by the polite phrasing that didn't disguise his order for them to leave. His whole attitude left her with the feeling that he belonged here and she didn't, that his orders were to be obeyed as a matter of course.

'Speak to me with regard to what, Mr Maddock?' she challenged, and sat down on the flowered sofa, leaning against the cushions to indicate that she was the one in her own home.

'This ranch.'

'This is a family holding, Mr Maddock,' Edie informed him. 'Alison and Jerry are directly involved in all phases of it. There's no need for them to leave. In fact, since it's the ranch you want to talk about, they should definitely stay.'

Briefly she wondered what he wanted to talk about. There had been no mention of a boundary dispute. Perhaps he had a complaint to make.

'A few weeks ago I made you an offer for this ranch,' he began.

'You made the offer?' she repeated. 'We did receive an offer on the property, but we didn't bother to enquire who made it since we weren't interested in selling it.'

'I was told by the real estate agent that you'd turned it down, even though it meant a quick and handsome profit,' Will Maddock admitted. 'I'm here to raise my offer by fifty dollars an acre.'

Edie raised an eyebrow in surprise, then

glanced at Jerry and Alison, who were expressing a similar reaction of astonishment. 'You're very generous, Mr Maddock, but we aren't interested in selling it.'

Impatience hardened his features. 'Let's not waste time, Mrs Gibbs. Simply tell me how much you want.'

If there had been any temptation to consider his offer before, it was gone now. 'I told you, we aren't interested in selling.'

'Everyone has a price,' he replied bluntly. 'You can use the money to buy a ranch somewhere else—one that isn't as run down as this one.'

'Considering its condition, you seem to want the ranch very badly,' she remarked.

'It joins my land,' he stated as if that was sufficient reason.

'Do you plan to own every ranch that joins your land, Mr Maddock? That would seem to be a never-ending goal,' she taunted.

His hard grey eyes turned to cold steel. 'It took years of neglect and abuse to let the place get in its present condition. I don't intend to stand idly by and let it go from bad to worse while a trio of greenhorns amuse themselves by playing cowboys.'

71

Incensed by his swift condemnation of them without giving them even the smallest chance to prove they might be capable of running a ranch, Edie rose from the sofa. When Will Maddock stood up to face her, she felt like a banty hen tackling a silver-tipped grizzly.

'I suggest, Mr Maddock, that you don't know us. You haven't even bothered to enquire what our qualifications or experience might be, although it isn't any of your business.' She was controlling her temper with an effort, speaking sharply and concisely.

'I know how much work it's going to take to whip this place into shape again.'

'We aren't allergic to work. In fact, we've been on a very intimate basis with it all of our lives,' Edie told him as Jerry and Alison moved over to stand beside her, uniting again.

'There's a lot of back-breaking labour involved, long hours of hard physical labour. I have no doubt the boy will do his share, or try. But two females?' His gaze flicked over them in obvious contempt for their contribution.

'You're underestimating us,' Edie insisted tightly.

His arm moved and before she could guess his intention, her hand was trapped in his paw. He twisted it upwards in front of her face.

'Take a good look at your hands, Mrs Gibbs, because a month from now you won't recognise them,' he told her. 'Your fingernails will all be chipped and short. There'll be calluses on those smooth palms. Your hands will be as rough as sandpaper. You'll be too exhausted to eat and too tired to sleep. And that's just the beginning!'

'We aren't made of glass.' She strained against his grip, but didn't struggle to free herself.

'You'll break.' There was a hard sureness in his voice as he released her hand. A numbness tingled through it as circulation was restored.

'Don't be too sure, Mr Maddock,' Edie replied, and refrained from rubbing her hand, not wanting to show any weakness in front of him.

It was a cruel smile that slanted his mouth. 'I'm sure of one thing, Mrs Gibbs, one way or another you're going to sell to me before the year is out.'

'That sounds like a threat.' She tipped her head back to challenge the man towering in front of her.

'I don't waste time with threats. You aren't hurting anyone but yourself by being stubborn, Mrs Gibbs.' He put his hat on and pulled it low on his forehead. 'Let me know what you want for the ranch when you're ready to sell.'

He started towards the door. After a second, Edie followed him. 'It's a pity that you didn't buy the place from Mr Carver since you want it so much,' she told him.

Pausing with his hand on the doorknob, he gave her a sidelong look that was shadowed by the brim of his hat. 'I was out of the States when he put it in on the market, otherwise you wouldn't be here.'

He left as he had come—without a hello or a good evening. At the sound of an engine starting up, Edie's knees began shaking. She hadn't realised how emotionally tense she had been. It was like shock setting in after the danger had passed.

'I'd sell this ranch to the devil before I'd sell it to him!' Alison declared.

'We aren't selling,' Edie whirled to correct that thought. 'Not to him. Not to anyone.'

'That's who Anson Carver was talking

about,' Jerry mused, staring thoughtfully in the direction of the car.

'When?' Edie demanded.

'When he said "the he-bull wasn't going to get what he wanted",' he answered with a faint smile deepening the corners of his mouth. 'I'll bet you Maddock tried to buy this place from Carver a half a dozen times and Carver wouldn't sell.'

'Why wouldn't he sell?' Alison frowned. 'Obviously that man Maddock would have paid more money for the ranch. Look what he's offered us!'

'I don't know. Carver mentioned a couple of things,' Jerry remembered. 'He didn't want the ranch gobbled up in a bigger one, which Maddock's obviously is. And he was glad we were going to be living in this house. Maddock would probably have torn it down or abandoned it.'

'You could be right,' Edie murmured. The old man had been a cantankerous, stubborn man. She doubted that he had sold the ranch because he needed the money, so his decision to sell to them might not have been dictated by price.

'This house is a dump and an eyesore. I don't blame Maddock if he wanted to tear it down. I wish we could,' Alison muttered.

75

'In time, we can fix it up.' Edie sighed, because she couldn't agree with her daughter more. 'But we have a lot more important things to do first. As Maddock would be quick to remind us if he was here,' she finished on a bitter note.

'You've had a rough day, Edie. Why don't you go take a shower and relax?' Jerry suggested.

'What about me?' Alison protested. 'This Cinderella hasn't exactly been idle!'

'Turn the radio on and prop your feet up. I'll do the dishes,' Jerry volunteered. 'According to Maddock, our hands are going to look alike anyway, so I'll give yours a break tonight.'

His remark teased an unwilling laugh from Edie and Alison, letting some of their normal good humour return. It helped dispel the doubts Will Maddock's gloomy predictions had cast.

'Nothing is very bad if we can laugh at it,' Alison stated, and they agreed with her.

CHAPTER FOUR

The next morning they were up with the sun. Packing some sandwiches for lunch and taking a thermos of coffee, the three saddled up their horses and rode out to inspect the property and its boundaries.

The tour around the perimeter of their ranch took the biggest share of the day. They made two discoveries, one of which Edie had already suspected. There wasn't a section of fenceline that didn't need to be repaired or replaced.

It was the second discovery that came as a surprise. Their ranch was bounded on three sides by Diamond D land. Will Maddock's ranch practically surrounded them. There was a stark contrast between his neat, precise fence rows running at right angles to the drooping and tumbledown excuse of their fences. Their meadows abounded with thistles while his were thick with nutritious grasses.

None of them mentioned the obvious differences nor acknowledged that Maddock had cause to regard the ranch as a plague to his own. Neither did they admit that there was more work to be done than they had imagined.

That night it was decided that Jerry would go into town the next morning and order the barbed wire and new fence posts while Edie and Alison explored the interior of the ranch property. They needed to learn where the best grazing lands were and their water sources.

No matter how much riding Edie had done in the past, none of it had prepared her bones and muscles for an entire day in the saddle and part of a second. By midday, she was so stiff and sore she wanted to cry. There was consolation in knowing that Alison was suffering, too.

These Dakota hills bore no resemblance to the Illinois landscape where they had ridden before. Here there were deep ravines to be descended and climbed, the horses plunging and rearing to claw their way up, rocky slopes to be negotiated, the horses' iron shoes slipping and stumbling over stones, and clear, cold streams to be crossed, the horses splashing the icy water on to their legs. Seldom was there time to admire the view. Daydreaming was usually punished by a low-hanging limb that the unwary rider didn't see in time to duck.

One such branch tried to decapitate Edie. 'Damn!' she swore under her breath as her hat was knocked off.

'Are you playing cowboys?' Alison teased, and leaned way over to pick up the hat without dismounting from the black mare.

'If you want me to laugh, use someone else's words other than Maddock's,' Edie retorted with a weary grin.

'I'll remember that,' Alison laughed, and returned her hat. They had ridden almost to the crest of a ridge. Alison reined her mare in a half circle to traverse the last few yards. 'Mom, look!' She pointed towards the valley below. 'There's cattle down there. Do you see them?'

When they rode down to investigate, they discovered a dozen head of Hereford cattle grazing in the tall grass of a meadow. The Diamond D brand was burned on their rusty red hips.

'What do you suppose they're doing here?' Alison asked.

'Eating our grass,' Edie retorted, and sighed, 'They probably wandered through a break in the fence. We'd better drive them back.'

'Our first cattle drive—and it's

79

somebody else's cattle.' Alison sent her a laughing glance. 'Too bad Jerry isn't here. We could outnumber them.'

Herding the cattle back to the boundary fence was a welcome change of pace. After an initial reluctance to leave the lush grass of the meadow, the cattle allowed themselves to be driven back to their home range. There were so many breaks in the fence, Edie couldn't guess which one they had come through, so it didn't matter which one they went back through. On the other side, they urged the cattle into a trot to chase them away from the fence, then turned and rode back towards the fence.

'Oh, oh,' Alison murmured. 'It looks like we're about to be caught trespassing.'

Edie looked beyond her daughter to see two riders approaching them. Will Maddock was one of them. No one could fail to recognise that muscular frame mounted on a rangy mouse-grey buckskin. The second rider was a girl, a wand-slim rider on a spirited sorrel with a blaze and four white stockings. Edie refused to hurry her bay gelding to reach their own land before Maddock intercepted them; they had a perfectly legitimate reason for trespassing on his property. A few yards

80

short of the fence the four riders reined their horses in to meet.

'Good afternoon, Mr Maddock,' Edie greeted him coolly.

He acknowledged the greeting with a faint nod, but didn't respond in a similar vein. There was nothing in his steady regard to make her so aware of her unflattering masculine clothes. Edie decided the sensation was aroused because he was so damned male she was automatically conscious of her own sex.

Her gaze broke away from his to study the girl on the prancing, restless sorrel. She looked to be the same age as Alison, but considerably more self-possessed. Hatless, she had a thick mane of dark hair, long and curling, and her eyes were an arrogant blue.

'This is my daughter Felicia. Mrs Gibbs and her daughter, Alison.' Will Maddock made the introduction.

'Hello, Felicia,' Edie acknowledged the introduction, and Alison echoed it. Like her father, Felicia Maddock simply nodded in response. Edie doubted if she was wrong to suspect that his daughter was a spoiled snob.

'Some of your cattle strayed on to our ranch, so we've herded them back,' Edie

81

explained the reason they were on his land.

'What can you expect? There isn't anything to stop them,' Maddock replied in a dry dismissal of the effectiveness of the dividing fence.

'I'm aware of that,' Edie countered stiffly.

'Good. Because it's your fence and your problem.' He was stating facts, neither taunting nor mocking, just smoothly pointing out where the responsibility rested.

Which was all the more infuriating. 'It will soon be remedied.' She was rigid.

'Let's go, Dad,' his daughter urged with undisguised boredom with the conversation taking place. 'You promised we'd go swimming when we got back,' she reminded him, and explained to Alison, with an upper crust dryness, 'We have a heated pool.'

Will Maddock's response was to tighten the grip on the reins. The big blue-grey buckskin he was riding showed how well trained it was by backing up in double-quick time and stopping the second the pressure on the bit was eased.

'You're looking tired after only two days, Mrs Gibbs,' he observed. 'You should get some rest.' His gloved hand touched the brim of his hat in a farewell gesture before he glanced at his daughter and reined his mount away.

As cantering hooves drummed the ground to sound the departure, Edie dug a heel in the bay's side to ride it through the gap in the fence. She was so choked with anger she couldn't speak. On their land, they both turned their horses towards the distant ranchyard, as if it had been previously agreed.

'Will you promise to go swimming with me when we get back, Momma?' Alison queried in pseudo-cultured voice. 'We have a heated pool.' It was a deliberate and acid mockery of Felicia Maddock.

'Didn't you notice? I'm tired. I need my rest,' Edie countered bitterly. She caught the glinting light in Alison's eye and, unwillingly, a laugh was pulled from her throat.

There was no sign of Jerry when they arrived at the ranch. They rubbed their horses down and grained all the stock. As they started towards the house, Jerry drove into the yard in his pick-up.

'The next time someone has to go to town, it's going to be me,' Alison announced. 'It always turns into an all-day affair.'

'Did you get the fencing ordered?' Edie ignored her daughter's jibe that Jerry had been loafing all day. They both knew better.

'I got it ordered all right.' He fell into step beside them. The grimness of his expression was echoed in his voice.

'What happened?' She knew there was more to that statement.

'I had to pay cash before they would even order it,' he explained.

'*What*?' Edie stopped, stunned by his announcement.

'Same at the feed store, too, when I stopped to buy grain for the horses.'

'Why? Didn't you open an account for us?' Edie demanded.

'I tried,' he admitted. 'But it seems we don't have any credit established in this area. We either pay on the line or we don't get it. The lumber company did say that if we stayed here for a year they would reconsider our application to open an account with them.'

'*If* we stayed?' Edie repeated in anger.

'That's what they said.' There was a wryly grim twist to his mouth. 'The word is out—no credit. It's going to be the same with every supplier.'

'And I can guess who put the word out,' she muttered under her breath.

'Will Maddock,' Alison supplied the name.

'He must have been laughing up his sleeve today.' Edie jerked the front door open and stalked into the house.

'Today? Did you see him today?' Jerry held the door for Alison, then followed them both into the house.

'Yes.' Alison explained about finding the cattle and running into Will Maddock and his daughter when they herded them back to Diamond D land. 'If his wife is anything like his daughter, she must be a real pain,' she concluded.

'She's dead,' Jerry informed them.

'How do you know that?' Edie glanced at him in vague surprise.

'I heard somebody mention it—at the feed store, I think. Anyway, I had the impression he lost his wife some time ago,' he shrugged.

Edie told herself she wasn't interested in Will Maddock's personal life. It had nothing to do with them; their problems were more immediate.

'When will the fencing arrive?' she asked to change the subject.

'Part of it will be delivered tomorrow. The rest they're shipping in,' Jerry replied.

*　　　*　　　*

The truck with the posts and wire came early the next morning. They elected to first replace the fence near the barns so they would have a place to turn the horses loose to graze. It was hard, monotonous labour—pulling out the old, rotten posts, putting in new ones, and stringing the barbed wire. Jerry did the phases that called for brute strength, but all three of them were staggering with fatigue at the end of each day.

When the area near the barn was re-fenced, they turned their efforts to the west property line where Diamond D cattle were wandering on to their land. The weather mercifully held, turning springlike with pleasantly warm afternoons.

As the sun and work started the perspiration flowing, Edie removed her jacket and tossed it inside the cab of the pick-up. Alison was farther up the fence row astride the buckskin gelding, roping the old fence posts, taking a dally around the saddlehorn to pull them out of the ground, and dragging them back to the pick-up to be returned to the house for firewood. She kept ahead of Jerry, who was setting new posts, and at the same time chased the curious cattle away from the fenceline, herding any out that wandered in. It was Edie's task to string the barbed wire and nail it to the new posts. Dipping a gloved hand into a sack in the back end of the pick-up, she scraped the bottom to come up with a handful of metal staples and slipped them into the pocket of the carpenter's apron around her waist.

'We're out of staples, Jerry!' she called in a tired voice.

Shirtless, the tough, sinewy muscles of his back glistened with sweat, dust turning into rivulets of mud to streak his skin. He finished tamping a new post, paused to remove his hat and wipe his forehead with the back of his arm. With long, tired strides he started back towards the truck, stopping to take his shirt draped over the previous fence post.

'I only have a half dozen posts left. I'll go back to the house for another load,' he told Edie. 'And staples for you. Have Alison help you.'

'She's busy,' Edie replied after a brief glance that saw her daughter spurring the buckskin towards some young steers racing with tails high through the downed fenceline and towards a distant stand of branch-bare cottonwoods. 'I'll manage.'

With the slamming of the truck door, Edie picked up the trailing strand of the top wire. Even with the protection of leather gloves she was careful to grip only the wire and avoid the pointed barbs spaced along the wire. Unwinding a long section from the reel, she strung it past one post and on to the second. There she tacked it to the far post and went back to stretch it tight to the first and hammer the staple to wood, holding it in place.

The pick-up was bouncing over the uneven ground, disappearing in the direction of the ranchyard when Edie remembered she had left the wire-cutters in the pocket of her jacket. Shrugging, she decided she wouldn't need them before Jerry returned anyway. With the top wire in place on the next pole, she strung the second and third strands, then went back to the top to repeat the procedure.

Tired and weary, her muscles hadn't quit

aching for days. But she had learned to block out the discomfort and, robotlike, focus her concentration on the task. As she tacked the top wire to a second post, there was a prickling sensation of danger along the back of her neck. When she turned to walk to the middle post to stretch the wire taut, she saw Will Maddock sitting astride the big grey buckskin, relaxed in the saddle and watching her. She faltered for a second in midstride, her pulse leaping in alarm that she hadn't heard him approach. Aware that his presence had been noticed, Maddock still didn't offer a greeting. Pressing her lips together, Edie decided if he could be rude, so could she, and continued to the second post.

'That isn't the way it's done,' he criticised with drawling indifference. 'That wire can pull loose from the far pole and whip right back on you.'

'It's my fence and my problem.' Edie tugged at the top wire to pull it tight. 'I can get along without any supervision from you.'

There was a curl in the wire that resisted her efforts. She leaned against the loose section, tacked to the far post, to get some leverage. Irritated that she should have any difficulty when Will Maddock was watching, she carelessly put too much strain on the loosely secured section of wire.

'Look out!' The barked warning came too late.

Edie heard a pinging snap, then there wasn't anything to lean against. She staggered for balance and heard the whine of recoiling wire. Sheer instinct raised her hands towards her face as the barbed wire circled her like a whip. A thousand needle-sharp points stabbed into her flesh, piercing her clothes to tear at her skin. She wasn't aware of crying out, but there was the echo of strangled screams in the air.

The wire had tangled at her feet, tripping her up and keeping her from regaining her balance. With each stumbling, staggering step, more flesh was ripped by constricting wire. Her attempts to unwind it only added to the agony. She couldn't even fall to the ground because the wire held her up. It seemed an eternity of time that she was trapped in the web of steel needles, writhing in pain, before a pair of hands held her motionless and gave her support. In actual fact it was only a matter of seconds.

'You stupid little bitch!' A familiar voice

was savagely swearing in her face. 'You were too damned stubborn to listen. You didn't want my supervision. Maybe you don't want my help either. Where's your wirecutters? I told you this would happen, but damn fools like you know everything!'

The barely controlled fury of his temper whipped at her, slicing into her pride the way the barbs cut her flesh. Yet all the while Will Maddock was berating her stupidity and stubbornness, he was supporting her with one hand and loosening the strands of wire circling her body. Each breath Edie took was a grunting cry of pain, the straitjacket of wire not permitting any movement without extracting a penalty of pain. Her eyes were tightly closed, trying to shut out the nightmare.

'Where's the damned wirecutters?' This time Will Maddock's voice demanded an answer.

'In ... the pick-up,' Edie whispered, and cringed in expectation of the barrage of abuse that would follow.

'Of all the—' The explosion stopped as the large hands on her arms tightened. 'Don't move,' his voice rumbled the order with thunderous warning. 'I have some in

91

my saddlebags. Just stand still and don't try to get free. Do you understand? Don't move.'

Hysterical laughter started to rise in her throat, because it was so ludicrous to think she could move. 'I ... can't,' she gulped down the bubbling sound.

When he released her, she felt a surge of panic. What if he left her? She fought it down as she opened her tear-blurred eyes to watch him eat the distance between her and his horse with long, running strides, and return with equal haste, a pair of wirecutters in his hand.

'Have you had a tetanus shot lately?' With his powerful grip he began snipping through the wire strands as if they were string.

'No ... I mean, yes, I have.' Tremors of relief were quaking through her as strand after circling strand fell away.

When she was free, he gripped her shoulders and lifted her out of the tangle of wire at her feet. Edie swayed unsteadily for a second, but his hands remained to solidly support her. His strength was a silent blessing. Edie tipped her head back to thank him.

'Maddock, I don't—' Before she could

express the gratitude she was feeling, he was cutting her off with a hard shake, angry sparks glittering in his flint-grey eyes.

'You stupid little female!' he raged again in a low growl. 'Do you realise how lucky you were?'

'Because you were here? Yes,' she nodded. Out of the corner of her eye, she saw Alison driving the steer towards the fence.

'No, not because I was here!' Maddock denied that above the noise of the approaching pick-up truck. 'That barbed wire went around your body. It could just as easily have wrapped itself around your face! It's a miracle you aren't scarred for life. It wouldn't have mattered who the hell was here! Do you understand?'

He shook her again and the blood drained from her face at his explanation. Knowing how easily the barbs had ripped through her clothes and into her skin, Edie closed her eyes at the thought of what might have happened if it had whipped across her unprotected face. Her fingers curled into the sleeves of his black shirt, feeling the iron-hard flesh it covered and gaining strength from him. Distantly, she was aware of the slamming of the truck door, but it made no impact on her until she heard Jerry's voice.

'Take your hands off her, Maddock!' he ordered, and grabbed at his arm.

As Maddock loosened his grip to send a fiery glare at her stepson, Alison came running towards her. 'Mom, are you all right?' Her eyes widened at the sight of the torn blouse and the blood oozing from the many cuts, and she turned on Maddock with a vengeance. 'What did you do to her?'

'I didn't do anything to her!' he snapped. 'Tenderfeet like you can do it all by yourselves!' With that, he was shaking off Jerry's arm as if ridding himself of a pesky fly and striding to his ground-hitched horse.

It was left to Edie to explain, somewhat shakily, all that had happened. While Jerry stayed to put up the fence, Alison drove Edie back to the house to clean the cuts and put some antiseptic on them. Only a few were at all serious, but all of them were painful. Her back, shoulders, and arms had suffered the most, but none kept her from working.

The following week it was decided that they had sufficient land fenced and could begin to acquire stock cows to build their herd. Jerry began attending the livestock auctions in the area. It slowed their progress in refencing, since Edie and Alison had to work at something else on the days he went to the sale barns.

After three weeks of regular attendance, Jerry didn't have a single cow to show for his efforts. His story was one of frustration. Every time he made a bid on a pen of cattle, the price went sky-high. Jerry dropped out of the bidding whenever the price exceeded the cattle's market worth.

The day of the next sale, it was decided by unanimous decision that all three of them would take a break from their gruelling work schedule and attend. It was a grimly silent trio who left their truck and trailer parked with the other ranch vehicles and walked to the sale barn. While Jerry registered and got his number, Edie and Alison went to the snack bar for coffee before the auction started.

The area was a hive of activity. Boisterous male voices hailed one another above the ring of the cash register and orders being given to a harried waitress behind the counter. The smell of cattle and manure permeated the room to make an incongruous mixture with the aroma of freshly baked cinnamon rolls and apple pie. Edie was standing to one side while Alison debated whether she was hungry enough for two rolls instead of just one. For a brief moment Edie considered the fact that neither one of them had to watch their weight, not the way they had been working lately.

'Hey, Cully!' Someone hailed the heavy-set man at the cash register. Edie glanced around in idle curiosity. 'You're in luck again today. That kid's here. I just saw him registering.'

The man took his change and turned to face the stocky cowboy, pushing his way through the crowd of hats and boots and Levi-clad men. 'That kid's slow to catch on, isn't he?' The man referred to Jerry as Cully grinned and pushed his hat back. 'Hasn't he figured out yet that Maddock ain't about to let him buy anything?'

Edie stiffened. To suspect this was what was happening was one thing, but to have it confirmed was quite another. She pretended to be interested in a sign over the counter, but every bit of her attention was centred on the two men, anger making her senses twice as keen.

'Sometimes I wonder how high Maddock

would drive the prices,' the cowboy was saying. 'I wish the kid wouldn't drop out so soon.'

'Don't wonder too much,' the rancher, Cully, warned. 'Hank Farber wondered that last week and started bidding. He wound up owning a pen of expensive stock cattle. Maddock shuts off his bidding the minute the kid does.'

'There's no question about it. Maddock wants that ranch.'

'Hell, I don't blame him. It sits damned near square in the middle of his place,' Cully declared. Alison started to say something to Edie, but she shushed her with a look and sent a glance towards the two men to indicate the reason. 'It's got some of the best grass and hay land around here.'

'After all Maddock did for Carver, I sure expected that old man to sell the place to him.' The cowboy shook his head in absent bewilderment. 'Carver never would have hung on to the ranch as long as he did if Maddock hadn't helped him out as much as he did. I know for a fact that Maddock made Carver a standing offer to pay a hundred dollars an acre over the market price. He could have squeezed the old man out of that place a long time ago, but he played fair.'

'Maddock is fair, I'll give him that,' Cully conceded, and grinned. ''Course, he can afford to be. That old man Carver, though, he has a streak of cussedness a mile wide. His idea of a practical joke gets a little twisted sometimes. Knowing how much Maddock wanted his ranch, he probably thought it was funny to sell to a widow instead.'

'That bothers me—I mean, her being a widow and all.' The cowboy frowned and shuffled his feet in discomfort. 'I've heard she's quite a looker. She's sunk her money into that ranch, trying to make a home for herself and her kids. They sure as hell are working hard trying to fix the place up. I saw them putting in new fence last week, all three of them. Maddock's kinda rough on her.'

There was grim satisfaction in knowing someone agreed that they were getting a raw deal. But the rancher Cully was laughing at the statement.

'Hell, Maddock isn't trying to cheat her, in the first place,' he declared. 'He's just trying to force her into selling to him. As for her being a widow, these females have

98

been screaming for equal rights—now they got them. If they want to play with the boys, they can't expect any special favours. If she can't handle the rough stuff, she'd better go back to the kitchen.'

'Yeah, I guess you're right,' the cowboy agreed reluctantly, and looked towards the door. 'There's Tom Haven—I've been wanting to see him. See ya, Cully.'

When the two men drifted away, Alison exchanged a look with Edie. 'We'd better go and find Jerry.'

He was in the auction area, halfway up the wooden bleachers that half-circled the sale ring. Edie and Alison hurried up the steps to where he was seated and whispered to him what they had overheard, keeping their voices low so others around them couldn't hear.

'There's no point in staying around here, then, is there?' Jerry concluded when they had finished, the line of his mouth thinning out.

'We know the cards are stacked against us, but I think we should play out the hand we've been dealt before we ask for a new deck of cards and change dealers,' Edie decided.

'What do you have in mind? Jerry eyed
99

her with a glint of admiration and wary amusement.

'I think we should let Maddock go on believing that his dumb tenderfeet haven't caught on to his game plan. Then he won't be expecting us to do anything else,' she replied. 'We won't talk about it now, though.'

'Okay.' He glanced at Alison. 'Where's my cup of coffee?'

'Oh, damn!' A stricken look of regret widened her eyes. 'I left it sitting on the counter. Somebody's probably taken it by now.'

'Thanks a lot, Sis.' He shook his head in resignation and started to rise.

'No, stay here.' Edie put a hand on his arm to detain him. 'They're bringing the first group of cattle in. I'll go and get you a cup.'

When the cattle were turned into the auction ring, it was a signal for everyone loitering in the halls and snack bar to come in at once. Edie had the feeling she was trying to go down an 'up' stairway as she edged her way down the steps against the stream of ranchers and cowboys going the opposite way. She was nearly to the bottom when she happened to glance up from the wooden steps, and straight into a pair of slate-grey eyes. The steps seemed to rock beneath her. The heel of her boot hooked the edge of the board and she would have fallen head-first down the last step if a familiar pair of hands hadn't caught her and lifted her the last foot to the ground. She was conscious of the warm, firm imprint of his hands making itself felt through the material of her floral blouse, and the sensation wasn't unpleasant.

'You'd better watch where you're going,' Will Maddock advised as he released her.

Her gaze flew to his tough male features, the light of battle sparking in her hazel eyes. 'That has a false ring to it, Maddock. Aren't you really hoping that we'll fall flat on our faces?' she challenged, and didn't wait for him to reply as she pivoted and fought her way against the current of the crowd to the snack bar.

CHAPTER FIVE

The morning after the sale, Edie leaned against the board fence of the corral and gazed inside at a pair of frisky calves.

Already several months old, the Hereford calves were already showing the hefty build indicative of their breed. The pair were the only cattle they had succeeded in buying at yesterday's sale. Crossing the corral from haying the horses, Jerry vaulted the fence to stand beside Edie and watch the skittish but curious pair of calves.

'It's up to you, Alison,' he said to the tall girl perched on the rail, 'to bring us home their mommas from Wyoming.'

'I wish you were going instead of me,' Alison sighed in apprehension.

'Maddock is convinced that Jerry will be buying our cattle. If he goes to Cheyenne, Maddock is going to guess that we're going out-of-state to purchase our stock cows. I don't know how long his influence will stretch, but I don't want to find out,' Edie replied. 'He'll never suspect in a hundred years that we'd send you to buy cattle.'

'Neither would I,' Alison declared.

'How many horses have you bought at auctions?' Jerry challenged. 'You know the procedures. Just make sure you get a health certificate and don't pay more than I told you.'

'I don't think I like being an adult,' Alison smiled suddenly. 'Too much responsibility!' She uncurled her long legs to climb down from the rail. 'Why do you suppose Maddock let us buy these two calves?'

'Guilty conscience,' Edie shrugged.

'He was probably afraid we might starve, so he let us have a couple of calves that we could butcher in the fall,' Alison suggested, and laughed at the thought. 'He doesn't know we have an income separate from the ranch.'

'Yes, Joe's patents. Maddock probably thinks we're depending on the ranch for our sole support,' Edie agreed, her dimples coming into play. 'Wouldn't you love to see his face when he finds out differently?'

'I was just thinking,' Jerry interrupted their laughter, 'I'll bet these calves are a carrot Maddock is dangling in front of our noses to keep us attending the local sales.'

'I wouldn't be surprised,' Alison agreed.

Edie rested her chin in the cup of her hand to watch the calves nosing a half a bale of hay Jerry had tossed in the corral. She tried to smother a convulsive burst of laughter and only partially succeeded.

'What's so funny?' Jerry eyed her curiously.

'I was just remembering all the grandiose

103

plans we made last winter.' She couldn't keep the laughter from bubbling in her voice. 'We were going to become big cattle ranchers. And *that's* the sum total of our herd!' She waved towards the two calves. 'It would take us longer to catch and saddle our horses than it would to round up and brand those calves!'

'I'm afraid you're right,' Jerry chuckled.

'We did say we were going to start small,' Alison reminded them.

'This small?' Edie laughed.

'Why not this small?' Alison challenged, making a joke out of it. 'We can start out with two, the way Noah did. Next year we'll have four, then eight, then sixteen. Why, in twenty years we'll have a herd!'

Both Edie and Jerry broke out in laughter. 'You have a problem with that theory, Alison.' Edie tried to check her laughter long enough to explain and failed.

Jerry did it for her. 'Those are bull calves!'

Then all three were overcome with laughter. Holding her stomach, Edie leaned heavily against the fence, tears streaming down her cheeks. The laughter was a release for all of them—a release from days of hard work, frustration, and tension. It turned something only mildly amusing into an object of hilarity. Alison fell against Jerry, laughing too hard to stand on her own. He circled an arm around her and reached out to draw Edie inside the curve of his other arm.

'Edie, you're the only person I know who can find something to laugh about when it looks like your dreams might be dissolving,' he declared in a laugh-winded voice.

'Neither one of you would win a prize at being serious,' she retorted.

'That's because of you!' Releasing Alison, Jerry circled Edie's waist with his hands and swung her in the air, lifting her above his head. 'You are the greatest, Edie!'

'Put me down!' she shrieked in laughter.

Jerry set her on the ground and planted a kiss on her forehead. 'I don't care who knows it,' he declared. 'Do you, Alison?'

'No.' The two exchanged a look that transmitted a silent message.

In the next second Edie was covering her ears as the pair of them tipped their heads back and shouted to the sky at the top of their voices. 'Edie Gibbs is the greatest mother in the world!'

'Help, you've stampeded our cattle!' Edie laughed as the calves bolted to the far side of the corral.

The helpless laughter was on the verge of starting again until Alison sobered with unexpected swiftness to stare behind them. 'Oh, oh,' she murmured in a small voice. 'We have company.'

Edie turned, wiped the tears of laughter from her cheeks. A blue and white pick-up was parked in the yard, the driver's door being held open by the man standing near it. Will Maddock shut it when they all looked at him. Edie wondered how a man could be so powerfully built and not look like a muscle-bound freak. He started towards them, and the three of them moved forward as a unit to meet him halfway.

A lazy smile was making attractive grooves in his sun-browned cheeks while his dark grey eyes were silvered with a glint of amusement and curiosity. Edie felt the magnetic pull of his male charm. Sexual and potent, it quivered along her nerve ends.

'I can't remember the last time I saw three people laughing so hard,' he remarked. 'What was so funny?'

Edie hesitated. 'It was a family joke.'

'I don't think you would appreciate the humour of it,' Alison added.

'Is this a neighbourly visit, or business?' Edie questioned to change the subject. The indefinable warmth that had been present now vanished as a wintry briskness took over the rancher's manner.

'Business,' he admitted.

'We haven't changed our minds about selling,' she told him.

'I didn't think for one minute that you would give up so quickly,' he murmured dryly, but his mocking look said they would eventually. 'No, it was another matter that I wanted to discuss.'

'Which is?' Edie prompted with an icy coolness.

'The below normal rainfall we've had this spring has hurt my grazing land. I don't want to risk over-grazing it, so I'd like to make you an offer to lease your land to run my cattle on,' he explained.

'But if we leased our land to you, where would we run our cattle?' she challenged.

'You don't have any cattle, Mrs Gibbs,' he pointed out.

'Not yet,' she admitted. 'But we hope to acquire a small herd soon. We already have two calves.' Let him think they were stupid

107

and gullible! she told herself. Anger surged when she saw the glimmer of a smile he tried to conceal.

'I think there would be enough pasture for your *herd* and mine,' he replied with mocking inflection.

Playing dumb didn't suit her. 'I don't think you want to lease our land because the lack of rainfall has affected yours, Mr Maddock,' she said, and was rewarded to see the faint quirk of an eyebrow. 'I think your land is overgrazed because it's overstocked. You've been buying a lot of cattle lately.' There was a slight narrowing of his gaze. 'We aren't interested in leasing you any of our land, but if you want to sell us some of your extra stock cows, we would be glad to discuss that with you. Naturally we would want to pay a fair market value for them, but you're a fair man, aren't you?'

He held her gaze for a long, hard moment. 'I'm not interested in selling my cattle at the moment.'

'It doesn't look like we can do business, then, does it?' she countered. 'Because we aren't interested in leasing you any land.'

'Very well.' Maddock accepted her answer with a brisk nod. 'Let me know if you change your mind.'

'Yes,' Edie agreed with a honeyed smile. 'And you let us know if you change yours.'

'Of course.' The slanting line of his mouth formed a smile of grudging approval, with a hint of admiration. Edie had a fleeting glimpse of it before he turned to walk back to his truck. Will Maddock had let her claim victory in this battle, but the war wasn't over. The war of the sexes was never over. A tingling shock ran down Edie's spine. Where had she got the idea that this was a man-woman struggle? That was absurd. It was the ranch they were fighting over. Will Maddock wanted it, and she was just as determined not to let him have it. It had nothing to do with sex.

Inadvertently she recalled the firm grip of his hands when he had caught her yesterday to save her from falling down the auction steps. And the previous time when he had held her supported while he swiftly and expertly dispensed with the ribbon of barbed wire. Unbidden, she remembered the warm, musky smell of leather, sweat, and horse mixed with the scent of shaving lotion. The combination was unique to Maddock, a stamp of his male individuality.

Even now, the virile scent of him lingered in the memory of her senses, honing them to a keen edge. Just for a second, she permitted a spark of curiosity to wonder what kind of lover he would be— masterful, knowing, both of those without a doubt. Like her, Maddock had been married, so making love would hold no secrets. But his hands, when they explored her body, would they—

Heat flamed molten-hot over her flesh when she realised what she was visualising in her mind. What was the matter with her? She had never indulged in such fantasies about Joe before she married him. She rationalised that away with the reasoning that she had been innocent of the act itself and hadn't been tempted to use her imagination. She was shocked that Will Maddock had aroused her sexual curiosity when not a single other man had—not even Joe who had been her husband and the one who should have.

'Why the frown, Mom?' Alison's question was light and innocent, yet it pulled Edie sharply out of her reverie.

Will Maddock's truck had completed its circle and was bouncing over the rutted lane away from the ranchyard. Edie was struck again by the abrupt way he kept entering and leaving her life.

'Just once, I'd like to hear that man say hello and goodbye,' she retorted.

'It would be a novelty,' Jerry agreed. 'Well?' He glanced at the two of them with a raised eyebrow. 'Shall we get to work?'

'Yes.' There was a grimness in Edie's agreement. 'We have a lot to do, and I want Alison to leave first thing in the morning.'

*   *   *

A violent spring thunderstorm arrived on the heels of Alison's departure. The deluge confined Edie to the house, where there was plenty of work to be done. Jerry used the time to work on the tractor which had been running roughly and make certain the haybaler would be ready when they needed it.

Intermittent rain showers stayed in the area for three days. The only ray of brightness came from Alison's telephone call of successfully accomplished mission and the date when the shipment of stock cattle would arrive.

The rain made preparation for the impending shipment impossible. Edie kept herself busy with the house, which had been neglected recently, but she would have preferred to be outside. All day long she consoled herself with the knowledge that the rain was needed. Proof of that was demonstrated by the way the parched ground soaked it up as quickly as it fell.

Yet, at night when she was alone in the front bedroom with the fingers of rain drumming on the roof, she tossed restlessly in the double bed. She finally tossed the empty pillow next to hers on to the floor, but it hadn't helped to ease her tension. Most of her married life, she had gone to bed alone while Joe had puttered in his workshop, so why did sleeping alone bother her now?

She tried to convince herself that these yearnings tormenting her were natural. After all, hadn't she read that a woman's libido reached its peak in the mid-thirties? Grief had no doubt suppressed these longings. Now that it had begun to wane, it was natural they would surface.

And there was a logical reason why the image of Will Maddock's face kept flitting through her mind. With the cattle on their way, she was subconsciously trying to imagine his reaction to the news. That was why she kept seeing those smoke-grey eyes look at her with such unnerving steadiness, those hard-cast features etched with strong, sun-creased lines, and that mouth cut in a male shape. These recollections had nothing to do with the brief flight of fancy her senses had taken the last time she had seen him.

Stifling a moan with her fist, Edie rolled on to her side and faced the empty width of the bed. Her hand reached out to the emptiness beside her. 'I did love you, Joe,' she whispered tightly. A little voice inside reminded her that there were many kinds of love and the force of one did not negate the strength of another. Many kinds of love existed side by side, one not diminishing another. She hugged the blankets more tightly around her and closed her eyes, listening to the drumming message of the spring rain on the roof.

The sun came out the morning the semi-trailer trucks arrived with the cattle. With Alison back and teaming up with Jerry, it was easy for Edie to forget her restive stirrings and join in with their jubilant spirits. Herding the cattle to a section of the range where there was plenty of grass and water was a festive occasion.

It was after one o'clock when they reached the valley meadow. Within minutes the cattle were scattering out to graze in the knee-deep grass, lush and green after the rain. Everything was washed clean, the air crystal clear, the colours of the trees and hills more brilliant than before. Wildflowers were bobbing their heads in the tall grasses and peeping out of rocky crags.

'Let's eat our lunch on the saddle of that ridge,' Alison motioned towards the hollowed crest between two hills, treeless and possessing an unobstructed view of the valley.

Her suggestion was quickly seconded by Jerry, and the three of them rode their horses halfway up the slope and tied them in the shade of a stand of white-barked aspens. Rocky boulders offered hard seats for them to sit on while they ate their plastic-wrapped sandwiches and sipped at hot coffee from the thermos. Yet the plainness of the food didn't alter the picnic atmosphere that predominated.

'I really feel like we own a ranch now,' Alison smiled.

Looking down at the valley floor where the mixed herd of Herefords and Angus grazed, Edie studied the shiny black hides glistening in the sunlight to contrast with the rust-red coats of the white-faced Herefords. She, too, had the feeling that what had long been a dream had finally taken the form of reality.

'We've worked hard these last months,' Jerry added in an equally quiet voice. 'But looking down there at that sight, it's quite a reward in itself.'

There was a clatter of hooves on stone behind them, and Edie turned to see a horse and rider top the crest and rein in. Unconsciously she rose to meet the silent challenge of Will Maddock's presence, a little pulse hammering in her throat.

'One of his spies must have told him about the cattle and he had to see it for himself to believe it,' Alison whispered in a caustic underbreath.

Except for a cursory glance at the herd grazing in the valley, Maddock exhibited no further interest in the cattle. His attention seemed to be focused on Edie. To enforce the impression, he guided his horse over the exposed rock face to where she was standing. He rested his gloved hands on the saddlehorn as he tipped his head down to look at her.

'The storm knocked down a tree on your fenceline. I thought you should know,' he told her. 'It's wise to check for damage after hard storms. Sometimes a small creek can turn into a raging torrent that wipes out a whole section of fence. Flash floods aren't uncommon here.'

The sting of his criticism smarted. Edie was well aware that he was taking the opportunity to point out how inexperienced they were. A trio of tenderfeet, he'd called them.

'It was thoughtful of you to come all this way to tell us.' But there was a bite to her polite response.

'I don't know if my reason could be described as thoughtful, Mrs Gibbs.' On that cryptic note, he turned his head to sweep an experienced eye over the herd of cattle below them. 'That's a fine-looking bunch. They're carrying Wyoming brands, aren't they?'

'Yes,' Edie admitted, and realised he could possibly tell her the name and location of the ranch that the brands were registered to.

The buckskin stamped a foot at a buzzing fly, and the saddle leather creaked under its rider's weight. 'You must have

made a quick trip to Wyoming and back.'
Maddock addressed the remark to Jerry,
who was leaning a hip against the boulder
near Edie.

'I didn't go.' Jerry calmly met the grey
gaze levelled at him. 'Alison bought the
herd.'

'Yes,' she piped up, a little smugly, and
strolled over to stand near her brother. 'It
was amazing how much cheaper the cattle
sold for there than the price they were
bringing here at the local sale barns. Even
with the shipping costs added in, we saved
money.'

'So now you're in the cattle business.' It
was a flat statement that ventured no
opinion.

'And we're going to be successful at it,'
Alison declared rashly. 'You shouldn't
underestimate the Gibbs family, Mr
Maddock.'

There was a suggestion of a smile around
his firm mouth. The glint in his eyes was
unmistakable as his glance encompassed all
three of them, lingering for a fraction of a
second on Edie. 'You can be sure I won't.'
Applying pressure on the bridle bit, he
signalled the buckskin to back up, then
pivoted the horse at a right angle to

send it up the crest.

CHAPTER SIX

'You're right, Mother,' Alison muttered in an irritated breath. 'It would be a novelty if he ever said goodbye.'

Edie dragged her gaze from the crest of the saddleback ridge where Will Maddock had disappeared. She had just begun to enjoy a feeling of peace and contentment before he showed up. Now she felt disjointed, at odds within herself.

'It doesn't really matter what he didn't say,' Jerry said, straightening from the boulder. 'He did give us some sound advice. We should check to see what damage the storm did. We might as well split up and cover more ground.'

'I suppose,' Alison sighed, and Edie let her agreement be a silent one as they walked down the slope to the trees where they had tied their horses.

Mounting up, they fanned out to take three different directions. Edie hadn't chosen the section of boundary fence she was to check. It had been made for her

118

when Jerry and Alison had chosen the other two. At the time there hadn't been any reason to object until she saw the rider walking his horse and thought of an excellent reason—Will Maddock.

Her gloved hand tightened automatically on the reins of the bay gelding. It pulled up abruptly out of its trot into a prancing halt. She glanced anxiously around her, but both Alison and Jerry were already out of sight. What was more, Maddock had already seen her.

Edie was angry that it hadn't occurred to her that this was the logical route Maddock would take back to his ranch. Or had it? And her subconscious buried the knowledge? It was too late for such thoughts to be occurring to her.

Her objective was to check the fences in this region. She had a choice of either following Maddock at a distance or riding on at a normal pace as if it didn't matter. It didn't matter, she argued silently. She wasn't afraid of him.

Digging in her heels, she sent the bay horse forward at an easy lope. Will Maddock didn't exactly wait for her, but she caught up with him easily. The ground became rough beneath her horse. Edie had

119

to let the bay choose its own pace or risk laming it, which meant she had to ride alongside Maddock.

'I see you decided to take my advice,' he commented.

'About checking the storm damage, yes,' she agreed stiffly, not turning her gaze from the front, but conscious of his grey eyes sliding over her. 'About selling the ranch to you, no.'

'I don't recall advising you to sell to me,' Maddock replied dryly.

'That's true,' Edie recalled with a touch of disdain that was alien to her nature. 'I believe you said we would break under the pressure.'

'You will, eventually.' He reached in his shirt pocket for a cigarette and, one-handed, cupped a lighted match to the tip.

'You're wrong, Maddock.' Edie tried to keep her gaze from straying to his craggy profile and the way his eyes squinted against the smoke curling from the cigarette in his mouth. He was too rawly masculine. 'I think we've proved we don't break under pressure ... even your pressure.'

'My pressure?' His mouth curved without smiling.

'Admit it, Maddock,' Edie insisted a

shade triumphantly. 'You're upset because we outsmarted you and bought our cattle elsewhere after you tried to keep us from buying any cattle here. You're irritated because you were bested by a bunch of greenhorns.'

'No, I'm not irritated,' he countered smoothly. 'And I don't deny that I kept you from making any successful bids on cattle. You can call that "pressure" if you like.'

'What else do you call it?' she retorted. When he didn't answer, she demanded, 'Did you really think it would work?'

'If you'd been a bunch of fainthearted, dumb tenderfeet—yes, it would have worked, because you would have given up in another month and sold out. You showed you were stubborn and intelligent. But it doesn't change the eventual outcome.'

'That's where you're wrong, Maddock.' Edie was angry that he was so damned sure of himself. 'We aren't selling. And if the day ever comes when we do, I'd sell it to the devil before I'd sell it to you.'

'And you're making a mistake.' He blew out a stream of smoke and gave her a long, hard look, his hands resting on the saddlehorn while his body moved with the rocking motion of the walking horse.

121

'I'm not making any mistake,' she denied, unable to withstand the force of that dark grey gaze.

'Yes, you are. You're taking this personally. I have nothing against you or your family. If you want to play cowboys, go somewhere else. I want the ranch. It's that simple. You have it. I want it and I'm going to do everything I can to persuade you to sell—to me.'

'Persuade? Force, you mean,' Edie corrected tightly. 'Doesn't it matter to you that this ranch is our home?'

'It isn't your home,' he denied that without hesitation or emotion. 'Wherever it is you're from in Illinois, that's your home.'

'That *was* our home. *This* is our home now.' Strangely, that was true. This was where she felt she belonged now. Their home and life in Illinois seemed a lifetime ago.

'Don't sink your roots too deep,' he warned.

The boundary fence was ahead of them. Blocking their way was a tall pine tree, toppled by the storm. Its trunk was charred black where lightning had struck it. The top third of it was resting atop the fence, a post taking most of its weight, which had

122

kept the newly strung barbed wire from snapping.

Ignoring Maddock, Edie reined her horse towards the tree and stopped near the fence. Since she had expected Maddock to ride on, she dismounted to untie the lariat hanging from her saddle. She glanced over the suede-covered seat of her saddle to see Maddock swinging off his horse.

'What are you doing?' she questioned.

'I'm giving you a hand.' He untied his coiled rope and walked towards the tree.

Hurrying, Edie reached it ahead of him and began tying the end of her rope around the tapered trunk. 'I don't happen to need your help.'

'I'm sure you can manage on your own.' He expertly tied his knot while she was still fumbling with hers. 'The same way you did with the barbed wire.'

She flashed him an angry look and jerked the knot tight. Walking back to her horse, she stepped into the saddle and looped the other end of the rope around the saddle horn. Maddock was already astride his buckskin, the rope dallied around his horn, and waiting for her.

Reining the bay at an angle away from the tree, she walked it forward until the rope was stretched taut across her thigh. Out of the corner of her eye Edie was aware that Maddock had set his horse at a parallel line with hers.

The bay felt the weight at the end of the rope, the resistance, and fidgeted nervously. Patting its neck, she urged it forward and looked back. Pine branches were making rustling noises against the fence. Slowly the top half of the tree was beginning to move. There was the splintering crack of wood as the tree trunk began to split from the lightning-struck stump. Then it snapped and the tree slithered off the fence and crashed to the ground, limbs cracking and breaking, the taut wire singing.

The rope went slack and Edie immediately halted her horse, its dark head tossing nervously. She ignored the fact that Maddock was already on the ground when she dismounted and walking to untie his rope from the tree. A white-hot tension was racing through her as she followed him.

Pulling the tree off the fence had tightened the knot. Edie had to work to get it loose. By the time she had it untied, Maddock already had his rope recoiled. His swiftness and adeptness made her feel clumsy and slow in comparison.

'I didn't ask you to help me, so don't expect any thanks.' She jerked the rope free and began coiling it into a circle.

'I don't expect any thanks. I didn't get any when I cut you out of that wire or when I saved you from falling down the steps. If neither of those warranted an expression of gratitude, this certainly doesn't.' His indifferent glance was cool and grey. 'Your manners leave something to be desired.'

'My manners!' If Edie had felt a twinge of guilt, his last statement chased it away. 'You don't even have the common courtesy to say anything as polite as hello or goodbye. You're too busy throwing your weight around! I imagine you've been pushing people around for quite a while. It's high time somebody started shoving back.'

'You?' Mocking laughter glinted in his look, although there was no change in his expression.

There had been too much tension, too many seething emotions held in check for too long. The thread of control holding them had worn thin. At this taunt, it snapped. Edie struck out at the male features that had tormented her in so many

125

ways. The leather of her glove absorbed much of the stinging contact with his cheek, protecting her palm.

Her arm had barely finished its arc when it was seized in a vice-grip. With a rough yank Maddock hauled her against his chest. His retaliation was too swift and caught Edie unprepared to resist. Her head was thrown back and her wide hazel eyes were drawn to his face. The white mark on his cheek was turning red where she had hit him. There was a thunderous shade to his grey eyes, a violent Dakota storm about to break over her head.

An instinct for survival made her struggle. With her free hand she pushed at his chest and strained against the iron band that circled her waist. It didn't seem to matter how much she turned and twisted, she couldn't elude the contact with his powerfully muscled body.

'Let me go!' she demanded angrily, and tried to jerk her wrist free of his grip, but he used the downward movement to fold her arm behind her back and force her more fully to his length.

'You did this deliberately, didn't you?' he accused grimly.

'I'm not sorry I slapped you,' Edie

126

flashed. 'I'm only sorry I didn't hit you harder!'

He continued as if he hadn't even heard her, anger blazing in his eyes. 'You deliberately provoked this so you could make me aware that beneath these boy's clothes there's a woman's body.'

'No!' she gasped the stunned denial.

She stopped struggling, suddenly conscious that the writhings of her body were a provocation in itself. She was no match for his strength. While he had easily checked her attempts to wrestle out of his hold, his hands had succeeded in fitting her intimately to the contours of his frame. Her hips were pressed firmly to the solid columns of his thighs and the thrusting angle of his hips. Trying to ease the pressure on the arm he had twisted behind her back, she had arched the jutting roundness of her breasts fully against his chest.

'How long has your husband been dead?' Maddock demanded. 'Has abstinence built up your sexual frustration until you can't stand it?'

A strangled cry of protest and denial was ripped unintelligibly from her throat. His accusation was too close to the wayward thoughts that had been running through her mind these last days. That knowledge flamed through her body. She had to escape him before his nearness caused a purely physical response. In a last bid for her freedom, she kicked at his shin with the pointed toe of her boot and scored a direct hit. He cursed in pain under his breath and relaxed his grip just enough for Edie to twist free. She tried to run, but he grabbed at her arm.

'Oh, no, you don't!' His fingers closed on her sleeve, catching just enough material to half-turn her around.

Her foot became tangled in the coiled rope she had dropped, and she lost her balance and tumbled backwards. She was conscious of her legs becoming tangled with his as she fell, toppling him with her. The impact with the ground momentarily knocked the wind out of her.

CHAPTER SEVEN

'You little hellcat!' Before Edie could recover her breath, Maddock rolled on top of her, capturing the hands that would have pushed him away and pinning them to the ground above her head.

Crushed by his weight, Edie couldn't move. Helpless in the face of his brute strength, she was conscious that the fall had knocked her hat off, spilling her hair over the ground. But she was more conscious of the pressing heat of his body and the way it heightened the earthy smell of him. She tried not to breathe and inhale his stimulating scent.

But there wasn't any way she could block out the feel of him, all that solidly muscled weight flattening her curves. It was too suggestive lying beneath him this way. She was afraid to move, in case Maddock discovered it, too. Her gaze became centred on the open collar of his shirt. She didn't dare look any higher, aware of the tanned column of his throat and the hard male features so close to her own. She could feel the warmth of his breath against her face, a sensual caress that she tried desperately to ignore.

There was a moment of stillness when neither moved. It stretched endlessly until some powerful, invisible force compelled Edie to lift her gaze. It travelled slowly up the corded muscles of his neck, dwelling for an instant on the pulse she saw hammering in his throat. For the space of another second, her eyes became fascinated by the strongly male outline of his mouth. Finally she met the magnetic darkness of his gaze.

'Will—' It was a plea, whether to be released or to be kissed, she never had a chance to find out for herself.

'Shut up, Edie.' The husky order was issued as his mouth lowered on to hers.

The shape of her lips was explored with consummate ease, every curve and contour investigated with sensual thoroughness. Her mouth became soft and pliant under the unfluence of his kiss. She couldn't stop the quivering response that trembled through her. There was a physical hunger that refused to be suppressed any longer.

When the sweet demand of his mouth seduced her lips apart, a languorous warmth invaded her limbs until they seemed to melt to his shape. A fever was born, contagious and hot. Her arms were released and allowed to find their way around the breadth of his shoulders. His arms forced their way beneath her and tried to absorb her into his flesh while he bruised her lips.

A blackness threatened to claim her.

Turning her head, she eluded his mouth and gasped for a breath. 'You're hurting me,' she murmured because she doubted that he knew his own strength.

Sliding a knee to the ground, he levered himself above her, completely removing his weight. 'Am I too heavy for you?' His husky voice was an evocative caress in itself.

Her lashes fluttered open as her gaze sought the face inches away from hers. She became fascinated by the sun-creased lines fanning out from the corners of his eyes and the slashing grooves that framed his mouth. She wanted to trace their paths as if they would provide the answer to the mystery of this man who could incite her to such anger—and such passion.

She could breathe again, but she didn't know if she wanted to. There was still his question to answer, and Will Maddock was waiting for it. 'Yes . . . I mean no.' She saw the satisfaction glittering in his darkly grey eyes as he watched confusion and desire chasing each other across her expression. 'Oh, Will, I don't know,' she admitted finally with a feeling that she had admitted a lot more than that.

'I never thought you'd be at a loss for a

quick, decisive reply. This is an occasion,' he declared complacently, and shifted his position to his length along her side, only a fraction of his weight resting on her.

His mouth moved to reclaim his possession of her lips, consuming them with a lazy hunger that fed her desire. She felt the smoothness of a leather-gloved hand cup the side of her head, a thumb sliding down her neck to the base of her throat. Then the caressing hand was abruptly removed and Edie was vaguely aware of some movement above her head. When the hand returned, it was minus the glove. The sensitive skin of her neck delighted in the pleasing roughness of his callused touch, responding to it the way her lips responded to the masterful seduction of his kiss.

Once his hand and fingers had explored every inch of her neck, his mouth followed them up to claim the territory as his personal property. His tongue seared his brand in all the sensitised hollows while his hand continued its discovery trail, pushing the collar of her blouse aside to investigate her collarbone and the point of her shoulder. Quivers of sheer passion trembled through her bones. Somewhere in the back of her mind a sweet turmoil was going on, but she was too conscious of the havoc his mouth was creating at a point below her collarbone. When he paused and lifted his head to let his fingers trace the area his lips had just claimed, she had to swallow a moan of protest.

'Is this mark from the barbed wire?' Will questioned in a low, taut voice that vibrated through her.

Edie moved a hand as if to touch the place, but the small scar was undoubtedly the result of that misadventure. 'I . . . yes.' What did it matter now? In this love-disturbed state, she wasn't interested in that incident, only in this one.

He pressed a kiss to the mark as if to speed the healing process and eliminate the blemish from her silken skin. 'I'll never forget that day and the sight of you trussed up like a little brown hen in that wire,' he murmured against her neck as he slowly worked his way up to her lips. 'After I cut you free, my first reaction was to wring your pretty little neck for getting yourself into such a predicament. So I did the next best thing by shaking you. But my second reaction. . . .' He spoke against her lips, tantalising their outline with the promise of a kiss while their breaths combined,

'. . . would have made the cockiest rooster proud. If your "protectors" hadn't arrived we would have been making love then instead of waiting until now.'

A tiny animal sound of pleasure came from her throat under the driving possession of his kiss. Phrases of his sentences began spinning in her mind. His hand had found its way inside her blouse and his fingers slid inside the cup of her bra to encircle her breast. His thumb teased the nipple hard, arousing her to the edge of total surrender.

No other man had made love to her except Joe. Will Maddock would be the first, and the experience promised to be like nothing she had ever known before. But wasn't it supposed to mean something? Did it? It was all happening too fast. Edie realised she wasn't ready for this—whatever it was.

With a muffled groan she twisted and rolled away from him, fighting the traitorous waves of regret. As she scrambled to her feet, common sense insisted that her decision was wise. What did she know about Will Maddock? What did she think of him? Was it loneliness that had made her respond, or something else?

'Edie?' His voice was low and questioning, puzzled yet insistent that she explain.

She realised he was standing—very close to her. The knowledge had a somersaulting effect on her heart and she took a deep breath to calm her panicking nerves. The action drew her attention to the unbuttoned front of her blouse. She quickly tried to fasten the buttons, but it was a fumbling attempt. She damned the gloves that turned her fingers into thumbs.

A hand touched her shoulder and she jerked away from the searing contact. 'No!' It was both a denial and a rejection. The next time he touched her, there was nothing gentle in the contact as Maddock forcibly turned her around to face him. Edie drew back, as far as his hands would allow, and refused to meet the cold steel of his probing gaze. 'Let me go, Will,' she requested stiffly. 'I'm not in the mood—' The rest of the sentence was lost in a gasp of pure pain when his fingers tightened to dig into her flesh all the way to the bone. She had been going to say she wasn't in the mood to argue, but he interpreted the words as they stood.

'Not in the mood!' he repeated in tight-

135

lipped anger. He clamped a large hand on her hip and yanked her towards him, moulding the lower half of her body to his length and impressing on her flesh how very potently he was in the mood. 'What am I supposed to do? Silently accept the fact that I'm to be sexually frustrated because a lonely widow has got an attack of cold feet? You let me become this aroused, Edie.'

'I know.' She suppressed a shudder of longing. Her aching dissatisfaction wasn't helped by the knowledge of his need. She hadn't intentionally led him on, even if that was the way it seemed. 'Let me go.'

For an instant, she thought he was going to ignore her brittle request. Then she was released and standing free, the subject of the accusing rake of his gaze.

'I didn't do anything you didn't want me to do,' he stated.

Unable to meet his look, she reached down to pick up the half-coiled rope near her feet. She concentrated on coiling the rest of it while she answered him. 'All right, I admit that I wanted to be kissed and fondled, but I'm not so desperate that I wanted to have sex with you.' Which was her fear—that she had responded to him out of a need to be loved as only a man can love a woman.

Her gaze ricocheted off his narrowed look. Turning, she walked to her horse and tied the lariat to the saddle. Raw nerves screamed at the way his eyes followed her every move.

'How long had you been married before your husband died?' he questioned.

'Eighteen years.' She stepped into the stirrup and swung on to the saddle. Feeling secure now that she was mounted, she glanced at him. 'Why?'

He had gathered the reins to his horse and mounted in one fluid movement. 'I was just wondering who wore the pants in your marriage—you or your husband?' There was something taunting in his steady regard as she squared his horse around to face hers.

'Joe did, of course,' she retorted.

'Of course?' A thick brow arched at the phrase. The saddle creaked as he shifted his weight deeper into the seat. 'I wonder why I have the feeling you told him what pair to put on.'

Resentment burned hot through her veins. She had made a lot of the decisions, but she had always consulted Joe. Will

137

Maddock's implication that she had been the boss irritated her. She refused to admit it was because it carried a grain of truth.

'I'm certain you wish I was a helpless female incapable of standing up to you. You would have had my ranch by now, wouldn't you?' she challenged.

He nudged his horse forward until his leg was rubbing against hers. 'Instead of wearing a man's clothes, Edie, you should try filling a man's bed.' The line of his mouth curved, but it didn't smile.

'Yours, I suppose!' she flashed angrily, and slapped the reins to her horse's rump to send it lunging into a canter which swiftly carried her away from Will Maddock towards the ranch house.

Edie didn't slow her horse to a walk until she was out of sight. She choked on a sob and forced it down. Her pride and self-respect were soothed by the knowledge that although she had been vulnerable to his attraction for a little while, she had overcome it. No doubt Will Maddock would be pleased if she was plagued by that brief interlude. It would be one more weapon he could use against her. Well, she wasn't going to let it happen. It hadn't meant anything except that she was human

138

and capable of being made to respond. She certainly wasn't going to hide from Will Maddock in the future because of it. After all, he was just a man.

★   ★   ★

Three days later, Edie was with Jerry and Alison on the south boundary, putting in the new fence. All the other three sides to their ranch had been re-fenced. When this was in, they could begin on the inner pastures, which wouldn't be for a couple of days yet.

At the sound of a horse and rider approaching, Edie mentally braced herself to meet Will Maddock. But when she looked up, it was his daughter who was reining in her horse. And she was alone.

'Have you seen my father?' Even as she made the imperious demand of Edie, her gaze was straying with cool, feminine interest to Jerry, who was shirtless, tanned muscles bulging as he drove a fence post into the ground.

'No,' Edie replied, barely pausing in her work. 'And I'm not expecting to.' Just in case there was some question.

'He said something abut moving some

cattle, and I just thought he might have been by here,' Felicia shrugged as if it didn't matter.

'I haven't seen him,' Edie repeated, injecting supreme indifference into her voice.

'Who is he? Your hired hand?' The haughty question was spoken in a voice deliberately loud enough for Jerry to hear.

'No.' With a sidelong glance at Jerry, Edie saw he had paused to look up, so she made the introduction. 'This is my stepson, Jerry Gibbs. Jerry, meet Felicia Maddock.'

The vibrantly attractive brunette walked her flashy chestnut over to where Jerry was working. An over-abundance of pride made her smile appear aloof, but there was no mistaking the avid interest in her blue eyes.

'Hello, Felicia.' Jerry's wide smile was natural, his voice was a little winded from his physical exertion.

'It looks like you're working hard,' the girl observed, and hooked a knee around the saddlehorn, leaning a hand on the cantle. The provocative pose was reminiscent of the kind from the Western calendars.

Jerry's gaze flicked over her in mild amusement, and a little interest. 'It's the
140

only way the work gets done.' He began tamping the post into the ground.

'Daddy is certainly going to appreciate all the improvements you've made on this place,' Felicia remarked in an attempt at adult cynicism. 'It will be just that much less he'll have to do when he buys it.'

'Presuming, of course, that we sell it,' Jerry reminded her, mocking her with his smile.

'You will,' she replied with false confidence. 'You can ask anybody. A Maddock always gets what he wants.'

'Is that right?' Jerry continued with his work.

'You don't mind if I watch you, do you?' Felicia questioned.

'No, I don't mind.' With that post in place, Jerry picked up his tools and moved on to set the next one. Felicia slid her boot back in the stirrup and reined her horse after him.

Alison pulled the barbed wire tight while Edie hammered a staple into the wood post to hold it. 'I wonder if Jerry feels properly honoured that Felicia is flirting with him,' Alison murmured in dry sarcasm.

Edie glanced in Jerry's direction. The other girl was leaning on her saddlehorn towards him, talking about something, but at this distance she couldn't hear what the girl was saying.

'She is an attractive girl,' Edie said, although she silently agreed that Felicia was out to make a conquest.

'The trouble is—she knows it,' Alison muttered.

Felicia Maddock stayed for about an hour. Not one sentence was directed at anyone else except Jerry. As far as she was concerned, Alison and Edie didn't exist. Although Felicia did the bulk of the talking, Jerry did respond at the appropriate times, but he didn't slacken his pace.

As she turned her horse to ride away, she tossed a mocking, 'Don't work too hard, Jerry,' over her shoulder.

'Don't work too hard, Jerry,' Alison mimicked. 'You'd better be careful, brother of mine. She wants to wrap you around her little finger.'

'Oh, yeah?' He paused to wipe the sweat from his neck, laughter twinkled in his eyes. 'She's just a kid.'

'She's eighteen if she's a day,' Alison retorted. 'And I wouldn't like to see her get her claws into you.'

'I think Jerry can take care of himself,' Edie inserted.

'Thanks, Edie,' Jerry smiled. 'To hear Alison talk, you'd think it was months since I'd seen a girl.' Then, with an impish wink, he added, 'Which it has been.'

'You just watch that girl,' Alison warned.

'I will,' he promised with a roguish grin.

Jerry had ample opportunity in the three days it took them to finish the fencing, because Felicia Maddock 'happened' to ride by every day. Each time she stayed about an hour, talking and flirting with Jerry, who neither encouraged her nor discouraged her.

Having the girl there automatically turned Edie's thoughts to Maddock. She studied Felicia, noting the similarities of their features and wondering if the differences came from Felicia's mother. Which prompted a curiosity about Will Maddock's late wife, and, ultimately, the question of why he hadn't remarried. With his virilely tough looks and status, there wouldn't be a lack of candidates eager to fill the position. But Edie didn't ask a single question, because she didn't want to admit an interest in him, not even a casual one— partly because the feelings he aroused in

143

her could be described as anything but casual.

Saturday was the day reserved for their weekly trip into town for supplies. The advent of June had also brought the annual influx of summer tourists to the area. The streets of Custer were crowded with vehicles and pedestrians. It took almost twenty minutes to find a place to park. Then it was several blocks away from the main business district.

'From now on, we'd better come to town in the middle of the week,' Edie suggested.

'You won't get any argument from me.' Jerry locked the door of the pick-up before stepping up the kerb to the sidewalk. 'Do you want to meet me at the hardware store in an hour?'

'We should be through with our shopping and errands by then,' Edie agreed after a questioning glance at her daughter.

'Most of them, anyway,' Alison nodded.

With the crowd of tourists filling the sidewalks and the buildings of the colourful Western storefronted town, it took longer than they anticipated. The hour had passed, yet Edie had acquired only half the items on her list.

'We'd better meet Jerry and catch the

rest of the things later, Mom,' Alison advised when they finally made it through the long line at a cash register. 'At this rate, it's going to take us all day instead of all morning.'

Jostled by a customer who was attempting to exit the store at the same time Edie was going out the door, she wasn't able to reply immediately. 'You're right,' she sighed with a trace of disgust, 'on both counts.'

They crossed the street to the hardware store and went inside, but they couldn't find Jerry. None of the clerks recalled seeing him, but the store was crowded. It was possible he had been in and already gone. They went back outside.

'What do you think we should do?' The corners of Alison's mouth were pulled grimly down by her fading patience. 'Should we wait here in case he's late, too? Or walk all the way back to where the truck is parked to see if he's there?'

'With all these people, we could pass him on the street and never notice him.' Edie frowned at the hopelessness of trying to recognise a person in this sea of faces streaming by.

'There he is!' Alison pointed across the

street. An eyebrow arched coolly. 'And will you look at who's waylaid him? Miss High and Mighty herself,' she declared at the same moment that Edie recognised Felicia Maddock as the one who had stopped Jerry to talk to him. 'I heard him mention to her yesterday that we'd be in town today.'

'Alison, you make it sound like she arranged to meet him,' Edie chided.

'I wouldn't put it past her,' was the shrugging answer.

Edie noticed the proprietorial way Felicia held on to Jerry's forearm. And she also noticed the smiling way Jerry observed the action, amused, indulgent, and not exactly indifferent. For a brief moment she wondered if the Gibbs family was naturally susceptible to the Maddock brand of charm. With a wide beguiling smile, Felicia said something to Jerry. His reply must not have been what the girl expected to hear because she abruptly withdrew her hand from his arm, her expression freezing in an attempt to hide hurt anger.

'It looks like Miss Prissy Pants had her fur ruffled,' Alison murmured with undisguised glee.

Edie flashed her daughter a reproving look, but Alison was watching her brother

146

cross the street to the hardware store. When he reached the other side where they waited, his gaze ran over them in apology.

'Sorry I'm late. I hope you haven't been waiting long,' he said.

'Long enough to see you with Felicia,' Alison murmured archly.

He glanced across the street in the direction that Felicia had taken. There was a wistful glint in his eyes that Edie noticed. 'Yeah, I talked to her for a few minutes,' he admitted without comment.

'What did you say that upset her?' Alison wanted to know.

'She asked me to buy her a cup of coffee and I . . .' Jerry paused, a vague frown clouding his expression.

'And—what?' Alison prompted.

A wry smile twisted his mouth. 'I told her that if I wanted to buy her a cup of coffee I would do the asking.'

'No wonder she reacted as if you'd slapped her,' Alison commented.

'But you wanted to ask her?' Edie suggested.

'Let's just say I might have if she wasn't . . .' He hesitated over the reason.

Edie supplied what she believed was the obvious one. '—Will Maddock's daughter.'

'I could have overlooked that,' Jerry corrected. 'What I was going to say is if she wasn't such a spoiled brat.' Adeptly he changed the subject. 'I hope you haven't finished all your shopping.'

'Hardly,' Alison rolled her eyes expressively.

'If you don't need her, Edie, I could use Alison's help. I bought a couple of gates and a metal water trough. The lumber yard is so busy that they don't have anybody who can help me load them,' Jerry explained.

'Sure, I'll help,' Alison volunteered.

'I think I can manage without her,' Edie agreed dryly.

'We'll meet you somewhere for lunch. That café by the corner?' he suggested.

'Okay. At one-thirty, after the lunch hour rush is over,' Edie suggested.

CHAPTER EIGHT

There was still time before Edie had to meet Alison and Jerry, so she wandered along the sidewalk beneath the shade of the overhang. A dress in a store window caught

148

her eye and she stopped to admire it. Made from a soft, melon-coloured fabric, its design was cunningly simple, revealing a lot of skin and shoulder while avoiding the plunging look.

Its obvious femininity made a mockery of the image reflected by the plate glass window. A slender, dark-haired woman looked back at Edie, her shapely figure covered in an uninspired combination of slacks and a knit top, a unisex-uni-age outfit. Her gaze strayed back to the dress that needed the roundness of a woman's body to properly show off both.

'Hi, Mom,' Alison's voice drew her attention away from the shop window. 'We were just on our way to meet you. What are you doing?'

Turning, Edie noticed that Alison seemed particularly vivacious, all radiant and fresh with an extra sparkle in her brown eyes. Jerry was with her, a typical hint of a smile in his expression.

'I was just admiring the dress in the window,' Edie admitted. 'Isn't it attractive?'

'It's gorgeous! It would look great on you, Mom,' Alison insisted the instant she saw it. 'You should get it.'

149

'And where would I wear it?' Edie shook her head, too practical to buy something that would end up hanging in her closet. 'What I need is a new pair of jeans. I'd get a lot more use out of those than I would that dress, beautiful as it is.'

'It is attractive,' Jerry agreed with their consensus.

'And you could wear it to the dance tonight,' Alison inserted.

'What dance?' It was the first time Edie had heard anything mentioned about a dance. Her gaze darted curiously to her daughter.

'Jerry and I had some time to kill before meeting you so we stopped at this bar,' Alison began.

Jerry interrupted to assure Edie, 'I had a beer and Alison had a Coke.'

'Yes, well,' Alison hurried on with her explanation, 'since it's Saturday night, they have a band coming in to play at this bar. Rob says they're really good. He's heard them play before.'

'Who is Rob?' Edie frowned in amusement.

'He's this really cute cowboy who was in the bar the same time we were there.' Which explained that excited glow

150

in her eyes.

'And this "really cute" cowboy asked her if she was going to come to the dance tonight, and made her promise to save a dance for him,' Jerry teasingly carried the explanation a step further.

'I think I get the picture now,' Edie laughed.

Alison looked selfconscious for only an instant before she shrugged it off. 'He might change his mind and not even be there tonight. But I still think we should go to the dance. We've all worked hard lately. It's time we had a night on the town.'

'I agree,' said Edie. 'But I don't need to buy a new dress to go to a dance.'

'You haven't had a new dress in years, at least not one like that,' Alison glanced again at the dress on the mannequin. 'Let's go in and see if they have it in your size.' She grabbed at Edie's arm to pull her into the shop. 'There wouldn't be any harm in trying it on. You might look terrible in it, who knows?'

When the clerk assured them they did have the dress in Edie's size, Alison took the packages from her arms and thrust them into Jerry's. Edie wasn't given a chance to resist as she and the dress were hustled into a fitting room to change.

Everything was perfect—the length, the fit, the colour, everything. She wasn't able to fasten the hook above the back zipper, but it didn't alter the appearance of the dress. She emerged from the dressing room, minus any shoes since her cowboy boots had looked absurd, to view herself in a full-length mirror.

Alison was busy looking through a rack of dresses with Jerry standing patiently to one side. She didn't notice Edie when she came out of the fitting room, and Edie didn't immediately try to attract their attention, too anxious to see if the dress looked as good as it felt.

For an instant she was dazed by the image of a slim, fully curved woman with burnished brown hair. The dress enhanced a natural allure Edie hadn't realised she possessed. It was as if she was discovering all over again that she was a woman—and liking the sensation. With a three-quarter turn, she looked over her shoulder into the mirror to get a back view of the dress. Standing on tiptoe, she tried to get an idea of what the dress would look like with heels. Out of the corner of her eye, she glimpsed the distinctive rolled brim of a cowboy hat. Automatically she assumed Jerry had noticed her and walked over for a closer look. She reached behind her back with one hand to try to reach the unfastened hook.

'I wasn't able to fasten the hook, but—' It didn't detract that much from the appearance. The material above the zipper simply didn't lie as smooth against her skin as it could. 'What do you think?'

'I think it's a sin that a body like that spends so much time in men's clothes.' The caressingly low pitch of Will Maddock's voice paralysed Edie. Her heart leaped into her throat, robbing her of even the ability to speak. There was movement as the reflection of his tall, muscled lines joined hers in the mirror. 'Let me get that hook for you.'

The pleasant roughness of his fingers touched the bare skin of her backbone just above the zipper, and the vibrations they produced shook her out of her trance.

'No. It isn't necessary.' She would have stepped away from him, but he already had a hold of the material of her dress. Knowing his strength and the fragility of the fabric, she didn't try to pull away and risk tearing the material.

153

'A man learns early in his life the mysteries of all the hooks, snaps, and zippers that clutter women's clothes,' he drawled in dry insinuation.

'Were you a slow learner? You seem to be having difficulty with that hook.' Edie was having difficulty keeping the breathless feeling out of her voice.

'The adeptness comes in undoing them. There isn't any need to hurry when a man is refastening a hook,' he told her smoothly as if aware of the effect his touch was having on her.

It was a combination of his touch and the task. There was something about having a man fasten a dress that made it heavy with implied intimacy. Edie's senses were reacting to that feeling. When he had finished, Will turned her to face the mirror. Their gazes locked in the reflecting glass. His lazy grey eyes took note of the wary and disturbed darkness of hers while Edie tried not to be aware of the way his figure-moulding clothes enhanced his attraction. The tempo of her pulse went out of control when he made a leisurely inspection of her length.

'A pair of shoes would add the finishing touch to the dress,' he observed dryly. The

154

remark pulled her gaze from his tanned features, so masculine and tough, so disturbingly attractive, to the bareness of her own feet. 'Don't you agree, Felicia?'

The mention of his daughter's name jerked Edie's gaze to the side where she encountered the girl's cold regard. For a fleeting second, Edie was surprised to see jealousy and resentment smouldering in Felicia's expression before it was disguised with a look of boredom.

'It would be an improvement,' Felicia agreed with marked indifference.

'Mother! You look stunning!' Alison declared in a breathy exclamation when she noticed Edie standing in front of the mirror, and moved away from the dress rack for a closer look. 'Doesn't she, Jerry?'

'It's beautiful, Edie.' His agreement was restrained, but no less sincere, as his attention was drawn to Felicia Maddock.

'I thought you were in such a hurry to get back to the ranch,' the girl accused with an attempt at hauteur.

'I don't recall saying that,' Jerry denied quietly, but firmly.

With a sidelong look through her lashes, Edie glanced at Will Maddock to see if he was observing this duel of will between her stepson and his daughter. He was watching them, all right, but the instant she looked at him his gaze dropped to meet hers. She glimpsed the light of challenge in his grey depths, but didn't understand its cause.

'I had a skirt that was being altered, so Daddy and I stoppd by to pick it up,' Felicia explained quickly, as if she didn't want Jerry to think she had followed him into the store.

'It fits you perfectly, Mom. You don't have to do a thing to it.' Alison shook her head in amazement. 'It's even the right length. Turn around so I can see the back.'

Edie pivoted selfconsciously, aware that her daughter wasn't the only one showing a lot of interest in the way the dress fitted her. She was shaken by the sensation she was modelling it for Will Maddock's benefit, seeking his approval. His gaze seemed to mock her with the knowledge when she unwillingly met it.

'You've got to buy it and wear it to the dance tonight,' Alison insisted.

She felt the faint narrowing of interest in Will's look, and her throat became tight, nerves tensing. 'No,' she said, and raised a hand in a shielding gesture to lift the curtain of hair near her ear. 'What I mean is

156

'... I don't think I'll go to the dance, so I don't need this dress. You and Jerry can go, but I'll stay home.'

'You are not,' Alison protested with an irritated frown and turned to her half-brother for help. 'Jerry, talk to her.'

'We've all been working hard, Edie. You need to go out tonight and have fun as much as we do,' he insisted quietly.

'We'll talk about it later.' Edie moved away from the mirror—and Will. She tried to sound light and uncaring, as if it was all unimportant.

'Miss?' Jerry motioned to the sales clerk for her attention. 'We'll take this dress.'

'Jerry—' Edie's voice was low and vibrating with impatience.

But he was too old to be silenced by the angry sparks in her eyes. The faint smile in his maturing face told her so.

'When was the last time you went dancing, Edie?' he questioned, and immediately provided an answer. 'It had to be before you married Dad, because he had two left feet and nobody could drag him on to the dance floor. We all had to gang up on him just to persuade him to take us out to dinner.'

Again she glanced at Will, who was

157

listening without any qualms. Jerry's statement made Joe sound as if he hadn't been a very loving husband, and she felt duty bound to defend him.

'I didn't mind,' she reminded Jerry.

'I know you didn't mind. That was Dad. We all loved him for what he was, not what he did or didn't do. I'm only saying it's time you had fun,' Jerry replied. 'And don't say you don't know how to dance, because you're the one who taught me.'

'I just don't feel like going.' It was a weak excuse, no matter how stiffly she issued it.

'Okay,' Jerry shrugged an acceptance. 'If you're going to stay home, Alison and I will, too.'

'Jerry!' Alison wailed in protest.

'You're both old enough to do what you want. You don't need me along.' Edie felt she was being unfairly pressured.

'If you don't go, we don't go,' Jerry repeated, and glanced at his half-sister. 'Agreed?'

A long, defeated sigh came from Alison as she nodded a reluctant, 'Agreed.'

'That's blackmail, Jerry Gibbs,' Edie accused. 'Emotional blackmail.'

'I think that's what it is,' he agreed with an impudent grin.

'Does that mean we're going?' Holding her breath, Alison glanced eagerly from one to the other.

'Yes,' Edie grudgingly gave in to the pressure.

'Oh, good! I found this darling yellow pant-suit, Mom. Let me show it to you.' Alison dashed back to the rack. 'I thought I'd treat myself to a new outfit, too.'

The sales clerk passed in front of Edie to hand a package to Felicia Maddock. 'I'm sorry you had to wait so long, Miss Maddock,' the clerk apologised. 'The alterations to your skirt took a little longer than we anticipated.'

'That's quite all right.' There was a briskness of dismissal in the reply as Felicia glanced over her shoulder. 'Are you ready, Daddy?'

'Whenever you are,' he agreed blandly, but Edie thought she noticed a flicker of irritation in his expression.

His daughter paused to flash an aloof smile at Jerry. 'Maybe we'll see you at the dance tonight. Daddy and I have talked about going. He doesn't like me to go alone because sometimes it gets a little rough in places like that. You could ride in with us, if you like. It wouldn't be out of our way to

159

stop by your place,' she offered.

Jerry was already shaking his head in refusal, but before he could voice it, Will Maddock was at his daughter's side, taking her arm. 'I haven't decided that we're going tonight, Felicia,' he stated.

Relief trembled through Edie. The prospect of Will Maddock going to the dance had filled her with all sorts of misgivings. Now it seemed likely he wouldn't be there, or he wouldn't have corrected his daughter. She wondered whether he was refusing because he didn't want his daughter chasing Jerry or if it was because he wasn't interested in running into her.

Felicia appeared unperturbed by his statement, although she surrendered to the pressure of his guiding hand. She smiled over her shoulder at Jerry. 'We'll see you tonight,' she said confidently.

As Will escorted her out of the shop, Jerry murmured, 'He should make her stay home on general principle.'

'I pity your kids, Jerry,' Alison declared. 'You're going to be a strict father.' She held up the pant-suit for Edie's inspection. 'What do think of it, Mom?'

'It looks great on the hanger. Why don't

you try it on while I change out of this dress?' Edie suggested.

'Do you like it, mean Daddy Jerry?' Alison teased him again about his sternness.

'Yes, I like it,' he agreed absently while sending her a sharp look. 'And I'm not being too strict. I just know our kids aren't going to turn out like Felicia—pampered and spoiled.'

'*Our* kids?' Edie raised an eyebrow in curious surprise.

It had been years since she had seen Jerry blush, not since his early teenage years. But a scarlet red was now spreading up from his neck to flame his face.

'I meant . . . when Alison has kids, and I have kids—our kids—we won't spoil them,' he tried to bluff his way out of that slip.

But Edie knew that wasn't what he'd meant at all. When he had said 'our', he had been referring to Felicia and himself. She felt a quiet rage searing through her. What was it about these Maddocks that could make you criticise them, find fault with them, dislike them even, and yet be so inexplicably drawn to them?

But all this escaped Alison's notice.

'You're right, Jerry. If any kid of mine started acting like that brat, I'd make sure they didn't sit down for a week.' She hugged the pant-suit to her. 'I'm going to try this on.'

Edie followed her to the dressing room to change back into her slacks and top and put her boots on. She pretended to accept Jerry's explanation for the time being. After all, who was she to give advice when she couldn't control her own wayward thoughts?

The only thing that needed to be done to Alison's pant-suit was that the legs needed to be shortened the width of the hem. The shop wasn't able to make the alteration and have it done in time for Alison to wear it to the dance that night, so Edie agreed to do it when they got home.

By the time they had had lunch, done their grocery shopping, and driven to the ranch, it was time to start choring. Chaos set in as they tried to fix supper, eat it, shorten the pant-suit, and all three have baths and get ready.

Edie was taking the last stitch in the hem of the slacks when Aliston rushed into the room in her bathrobe. 'Mom, help me. I washed my hair and now I can't do a thing with it!' The styling dryer was in one hand, a brush and curling wand in the other.

'How long is this going to take?' Jerry asked with a sigh. Already dressed in a forest green leisure suit, he was sitting on the couch, twirling his hat in his hand in an attempt at patience.

'You can't expect me to go looking like this,' Alison defended.

'It wouldn't make a very good impression on that cute cowboy Rob, would it?' he grinned. She wrinkled her nose at him, then laughed. 'Edie still has to get dressed and you still have to put your make-up on. I'm going to go to sleep waiting for you guys.' He straightened. 'If it's okay, I'm going into town now. You folks can drive the car. I'll take the truck.'

'Go on ahead,' Edie agreed, and knotted the hem thread. 'It may take us a while.'

'If you don't come with Alison I'll drive back out here for you,' Jerry warned.

'I'll be there,' she promised.

'Save us a table,' Alison called after him as he walked to the door.

'If you aren't there by midnight, the table is liable to turn into a pumpkin.' Then the door was slamming behind him.

It was nearly an hour later before they

left the ranch. The late setting summer sun was just dipping below the horizon when they reached the outskirts of Custer. There wasn't any place to park near the bar, but they finally found a spot more than a block away.

The bar was typically dimly lit and crowded with people. Amplifiers, positioned strategically throughout the room, blared with the country music being played by the band on the small stage. Jerry saw them before they ever noticed him in the multitude of people. As Edie wound her way through the maze of tables and chairs ahead of Alison to the one near the dance floor, she realised there was another man with Jerry. Alison was quick to identify him as Rob Lydell, her cowboy.

'We were just about to send out a search party for you two,' Jerry shouted above the din of music and voices, then managed an introduction to the young but sun-aged cowboy, who possessed an engaging smile.

The waitress stopped at their table. Jerry and Rob ordered two more beers, but Edie elected to have a Coke, the same as Alison. At first it was difficult to hear the conversation, but she gradually learned to syphon out the other sounds and listen only to those at her table. They laughed and talked, then Rob asked Alison to dance.

'He seems nice,' Edie observed as she watched the pair circling the crowded dance floor.

'I like him—which is more than I could say for some of Alison's choices,' Jerry agreed with a rueful smile. 'Like loverboy Craig.'

'I try not to remember him,' Edie murmured.

When the band finished the ballad, they went immediately into an up-temp tune. The couple stayed on the floor to dance to it. After that song was over, the band took a twenty-minute break. Edie tried not to notice that Rob's chair had slid closer to Alison's when they came back to sit at the table.

Some of Rob's friends stopped by to talk as a jukebox took over for the band. Edie was glad that they had come to the dance. Jerry and Alison were meeting more people in this one night than they had met since they had moved here. They should have begun socialising sooner, only there had been so much work to do.

As the band returned to the small stage after their break, Edie leaned forward to mention her thought to Jerry. His attention was focused on the dance floor when he suddenly looked very tense. He appeared to force himself to relax. Curious, Edie followed the direction of his gaze and saw Felicia Maddock dancing with some cowboy. At that moment, the girl glanced towards their table and feigned a look of surprise.

'Hi, Jerry!' She waved and smiled a greeting that was much too casual. 'I told you I'd see you tonight.' Then she was being whirled into the centre of the floor by her partner.

'Little Miss-Nose-in-the-air can't even say hello to me,' Alison grumbled in irritation.

'She's like that sometimes,' Rob admitted. 'But she isn't really a bad kid.' Then as if he realised his opinion didn't exactly please Alison, he let the subject drop.

Jerry made no comment, although Edie noticed his gaze kept straying to the dance floor, keeping track of the young brunette. But he wasn't nearly as talkative as he had been before. For that matter, neither was she. If Felicia was here, so was her father. Unconsciously, Edie kept searching for him

166

until she saw him standing at the counter bar.

There was an understated simplicity to his clothes—a white shirt unbuttoned at the throat and a buckskin vest hanging open. The Western cut of his brown slacks fitted closely to his hips and legs, flaring slightly over his boots with their underslung rider's heels. He was engaged in conversation with a cowboy standing beside him. When his head turned in the direction of the dance floor, Edie looked immediately away, not wanting to be caught looking at him.

Aware of his presence as she was, it was impossible to keep her gaze from straying to him. Yet Will Maddock didn't seem to notice her at all. She did a poor job of convincing herself that she was glad.

Alison was in high spirits as she returned to the table hand in hand with her cowboy. Her face was aglow. To Edie, her daughter seemed to be floating on air. She felt a tiny bit envious when Alison drifted on to the chair beside her.

Rob didn't immediately sit down. 'Want another beer, Jerry?'

Jerry seemed to have a hard time assimilating the question, not answering until he had torn his gaze from the couples

167

leaving the dance floor. 'Yeah, I'll have another,' he agreed, drawing a deep breath.

'Would you like another Coke, Alison?' Rob enquired, and received an affirmative and smiling nod. His glance then sought out Edie. 'How about you, Mrs Gibbs?'

The appellation made her feel extraordinarily old. 'No, thank you,' she refused.

The cowboy had barely left the table before Alison was leaning excitedly towards her. 'Rob wants to take me home. Do you think it's all right, Mom?'

'I've only just met him, Alison,' Edie protested. 'I don't know anything about him. Neither do you.'

'He's nice—you can see that.' Alison was at her persuasive best. 'What shall I tell him?'

Maternal instinct insisted that Edie order Alison to come home with her, but it was overwhelmed by the memory of Rob's voice referring to her as Mrs Gibbs. Her sigh was almost inaudible.

'I can't give you an answer just yet. You can't expect me to make a spur-of-the-moment decision like that, Alison. Let me think about it,' she insisted with a vague smile of reassurance.

168

'But what if he asks me?' her daughter frowned anxiousy.

'Let him dangle a little,' Edie shrugged. 'Tell him he'll have to wait and see.'

With a grimacing sigh, Alison straightened to glance at the returning cowboy and smile a quick welcome. Edie inspected Rob with a closer eye. Her conclusion matched Jerry's. Rob Lydell was an improvement on some of Alison's past choices in boy-friends.

She didn't notice Jerry rise to his feet until he touched her arm. 'The band is playing a slow song, Edie. Want to dance?'

'I'd love to,' she agreed without hesitation, and straightened from her chair. 'It's been ages since I've danced, so if I step on your toes, don't complain,' she added as Jerry guided her on to the dance floor.

'I'm not worried about you stepping on my toes,' he grinned. 'After all, you're the one who taught both me and Alison how to dance.' He turned her into his arms.

CHAPTER NINE

Within seconds after they had joined the other couples on the dance floor, Jerry became silent and his expression grew serious. Edie glanced around to find the source of his distraction. She knew she had located it the instant her gaze found Felicia dancing with her father. Edie looked quickly away, but not before her heart did a succession of flips at the sight of Will Maddock.

All her senses were on guard, alerted now to the rancher's presence and tracking him with some inbuilt kind of radar. When someone brushed a shoulder against hers, she didn't have to turn to know who it was.

Confirmation came with the stiffening of Jerry's arm around her waist and the low pitch of Will Maddock's familiar voice as he suggested, 'Why don't we change partners?'

Edie couldn't think of a single logical reason to refuse, especially when Jerry was releasing her to welcome Felicia. Then Will's large hand was on her waist and Edie found herself being guided into his arms and matching her steps to the simple pattern of his. When she lifted her gaze to his rugged face, his grey eyes were smiling at her in a knowing fashion, as if he was aware of the disturbing effect he had on her. Yet Edie suspected it was all her imagination.

When his gaze drifted after the couple dancing away from them, she glanced at them too. The young pair were completely wrapped up in each other, oblivious to everything else around them.

'Young love.' There was a dryness to Will's remark and it glittered in his eyes when Edie glanced at them. 'No one could pay me to go through those throes of agony again.'

In spite of herself, she smiled. 'Nor me.' She was conscious of a very comfortable closeness, something warm and wonderful.

'My daughter is a true Maddock,' he observed in the same tone as before. 'Once she decides she wants something, she goes after it. I'm afraid she's decided she wants your stepson.'

'Jerry is of the opinion that she has some growing up to do,' Edie replied. 'At the moment he finds her spoiled, self-centred, and immature.'

There was agreement in his throaty chuckle. 'I always believed that boy had a head on his shoulders even if he is caught up in that dream of yours about the ranch.' Before Edie could take offence at his remark, he continued, 'That's the trouble with being an only parent. It's hard to say "no". I keep trying to make up for the fact that she doesn't have a mother. Normally I wouldn't approve of Felicia being with someone Jerry's age, but I'm hoping he'll gently teach her that she can't always have her way.'

His arm tightened around her waist as he avoided a collision with another couple. It broke the pattern and Edie missed a step and brushed against him. The contact with the hard-muscled flesh of his length brought an instant recall of other times when she had been held this close. She had accepted the fact that she found him sexually attractive, but she was only just beginning to discover that he aroused her emotionally, too. Its existence was strong at this moment as his hand shaped itself to the small of her back.

She resisted the moulding pressure of his hand, as she resisted the discovery of her growing emotional involvement. Directing

172

her gaze away from the broad set of his shoulders and the tanned column of his throat, she sought the distraction of other couples on the dance floor. Alison was among them, her arms wrapped around the neck of her partner.

'Will, do you know anything about that cowboy dancing with Alison?' She drew his attention to the pair. 'His name is Rob Lydell.'

'Yes, I know him. What about him?' His glance was curious.

'He's asked to give Alison a ride home tonight,' she explained. 'I've only just met him and I wasn't sure whether I should let Alison go with him or not.'

The corners of his mouth twitched in an attempt to suppress a smile. 'I think it's safe to say you can trust him.' His tone and his vaguely amused attitude caused Edie to frown in confusion. 'Rob works for me,' he revealed. At first she was too stunned by his answer to reply.

'I should have guessed,' she murmured almost under her breath. What was there about these Maddocks? she wondered. First Jerry was succumbing to his daughter's charm and Alison was all wrapped up with one of his hired hands.

173

And here she was, caught up in some crazy longing for the rancher himself.

'If you'd like, I'll have a talk with Rob and make certain you have no cause for concern about Alison,' he offered with parental understanding.

'It isn't that.' She shook her head, impatient and suddenly defensive. She attacked out of instinct. 'Why can't you leave us alone?'

His glinting grey eyes ran over her face, following her thoughts, and the line of his mouth became mocking. 'You know the old saying—If you can't fight them, join them.'

It wasn't meant to be taken seriously, she realised. He was only baiting her, trying to get a rise from her. Well, she wasn't going to give him the satisfaction. Her gaze was fixed on a point beyond his shoulder. Will uncurled his fingers from around her hand and tucked one under her chin, lifting it. She was forced to meet his steady grey eyes.

'We Maddocks aren't such a bad lot, Edie. You've got the wrong impression of us altogether,' he told her. 'Our differences have been on a purely business level. Your mistake was taking it personally. I've told you that before, but you still don't believe me. Your ranch happens to sit on land I

174

want. If you'd bought any other place, I would have wished you the best of luck.'

His fingers slowly stroked the underside of her jaw, tracing its firm set. Edie closed her eyes at the raw ache his caress induced, and her fingers closed over his forearm to draw his hand away as the music stopped.

'Which doesn't change the fact that we still own the ranch, and we aren't going to sell it to anyone,' she replied tightly.

Turning out of his arm, she left the dance floor to return to her table. She was conscious that he followed her, escorting her back. At the table, he pulled out her chair. As she sat down, both Jerry and Alison returned. Edie looked up to see the measured look Will gave the two before he nodded briefly to her and moved away towards the bar.

'You didn't mind changing partners, did you, Edie?' Jerry studied the stillness of her features with an anxious frown.

'Of course not.' Her assuring smile was stiff, not fully natural.

But Jerry didn't seem to notice as his gaze travelled after the rancher, seeking him out among the others lined up at the bar. 'What do you think Maddock would say if I asked to take Felicia home?'

175

'I'm sure you would have his permission,' she replied, remembering the approval Will had voiced about Jerry.

'Did he say anything about Felicia and me while you were dancing?' Jerry was quick to catch the note of certainty in her tone.

'Yes. Something to the effect that Felicia has made up her mind she wants you—and a Maddock always gets what he or she wants. So I don't think your request will come as any surprise to him.' She smiled to take the little sting of bitterness out of her words.

But Jerry hadn't noticed it. 'Excuse me,' he rose from his chair to make his way through the crowd to Felicia.

'I don't know what he sees in her,' Alison muttered. 'She's a brat.'

'But a very beautiful brat,' Edie pointed out, then remarked on the absence of her daughter's suitor. 'Where's Rob?'

'He stopped to chat with some friends. He'll be here shortly,' Alison replied confidently.

'You didn't mention that he worked for Will Maddock.' Edie observed the way her daughter nibbled at her lip, revealing that the information had been known to her.

176

'Just because he works for them, that doesn't make him like them,' she reasoned. 'Rob is nice.'

'I'm not going to argue with that. If you want to ride home with him, I have no objection.' After all, Will had vouched for him and it was obviously what Alison wanted.

'Thanks, Mom!' Her face was wreathed by a smile as she leaned over to give Edie a quick hug.

Rob returned to the table to sit beside Alison and Edie was forgotten as the two spoke in low voices to each other. With Jerry gone as well, Edie felt superfluous. Everyone was paired up except her, and she didn't like the lonely feeling that gave her.

Rising, she laid a hand on her daughter's shoulder to intrude gently on their conversation. 'I'm going home,' she explained the reason for the interruption.

'You can't leave now, Mom,' Alison protested. 'It's early yet.'

'Maybe for you, but it's late for me.' She glanced at the young man sitting so close to her daughter and smiled. 'Goodnight, Rob.'

'Goodnight, ma'am. I'll see that Alison gets home safely,' he promised.

177

'I won't be late,' Alison added.

'Tell Jerry I've left when you see him,' said Edie as she moved away from the table towards the door.

Outside the music and the noise of the bar was muffled. Edie paused and lifted her gaze to the night sky, brilliant with stars. A big, heavy moon lolled above the jagged horizon of the Black Hills. After the smoke-filled bar, the air smelled fresh and sweet.

As her thoughts wandered over the night's events, she strolled in the direction where they had left the car parked. What was it the master battle tacticians said? Divide and conquer. That was precisely what was happening. Jerry was with Felicia Maddock. Alison was with Rob Lydell, Maddock's hired man. And she was finding Will Maddock more irresistible with each meeting. It didn't bode well for the future.

She sighed and crossed in front of the dark opening to an alleyway. With her head down, she didn't notice that the next building contained a honky-tonk bar until the door slammed and three laughing cowboys staggered outside. They dawdled there, trying to decide where to go next. They were blocking the front part of the sidewalk, so Edie moved to walk behind them and continue to her car parked a half block way. At that moment they noticed her and one of them let out a long wolf whistle. The implied compliment tugged at the corners of her mouth with a smile.

'Where are you going, honey?' One of the young cowboys moved in front of her to stop her.

'Can we come along?' A second spoke up.

The building was at her back as they crowded around her, yet there was nothing threatening in their manner. They'd had a few drinks and were ready for a good time. Edie was neither worried nor afraid.

'Sorry, fellers. I'm on my way home, so how about letting me by?' Her request was friendly but firm.

'The night's young,' the third insisted. 'It's too early to go home.'

'I'll bet she had a fight with her boy-friend,' the first one guessed.

The second cowboy took up the thought before Edie could respond. 'You aren't going to let him spoil your evening, are you? It would be a shame to let that pretty dress go to waste.'

'We'll take you out,' the first one offered. 'You just tell us where you want to go and we'll take you.' There was a chorus of agreement from the other two.

'Thanks for the invitation, but I want to go home—*alone*,' she stressed the last to leave them in no doubt. 'Would you mind letting me pass?'

There was a slight shift, creating a gap between the two of them. As Edie started to slip through it, the third cowboy made one last attempt to change her mind.

'Come on, honey, take pity on three lonely cowboys,' he coaxed.

A voice came from behind all of them. 'You boys aren't listening. The lady said "no".'

Edie pivoted as she recognised Will Maddock's voice. The sight of his large frame standing by the shadows of the alleyway took everyone by surprise. The young cowboy closest to him recovered first and swaggered forward a couple of steps.

'Well, well, well, if it ain't the big bull of the woods himself,' he drawled with exaggerated thickness. 'I don't recall you bein' invited to this party.'

'I invited myself. Now let the lady pass.' There was a steel-hard quality to his voice, but his face was in the shadows, and Edie couldn't make out his features.

180

The third cowboy continued to stand in front of Maddock in silent challenge. 'Is that an order?'

'Yes.'

Edie felt the tension build in the air. These boys were ripe for some excitement and Will Maddock's attitude was all the provocation they needed. She could sense it rippling through the trio of cowhands out for a night on the town.

'What if we don't obey your order?' the freckle-faced one on Edie's left asked with feigned innocence.

'I guess I'll have to show you that it's the right thing to do,' Will Maddock shrugged easily.

'Will—' Edie attempted to protest about his handling of the situation, but he didn't give her a chance.

'Stay out of this, Edie,' he ordered tersely.

'Edie?' The second cowhand looked at her, catching his familiar use of her name and drawing his own conclusion. 'Is he the one who spoiled your evening and sent you home early?'

She intended to respond to that and attempt to defuse the scene, but it had already escalated beyond the point where

181

any of the men would listen to her. She realised that as soon as the first cowboy took a step towards Will.

'I always wondered if you were as tough as everyone says,' he drawled. 'I guess I'll have to find out for myself.'

'I guess you will,' Will agreed.

The cowboy took the first swing, a blow that was warded off by Will Maddock's upraised arm. With every intention of stopping the fight before it went further, Edie took a step forward, but the shortest cowboy of the trio caught her by the waist to prevent her from reaching the scuffling pair.

'You'd better stay here, miss,' he advised for her own protection. 'We don't want you getting hurt.'

Despite her struggles, she was held fast. When it became apparent that the first cowboy was getting the worst of it, the freckle-faced cowboy rushed in to help his buddy. The cowboy holding Edie blocked most of her view, limiting her knowledge of the fight to the grunting sounds of the protagonists and the thud of landing fists and thrashing bodies.

Finally there was a kind of silence underlined with heavy breathing and punctuated with soft moans. The arms holding Edie loosened as the last cowboy carefully let her go and moved out of her way. She saw Will standing there, breathing hard and swaying a little while his two opponents staggered unsteadily to their feet.

'Had enough?' His rough voice made a winded challenge.

One of them nodded an affirmative answer and reached down to scoop up Will's hat and hand it to him. Edie stared in stunned disbelief as the cowboy's hand remained outstretched to shake Will's. The second cowboy did the same in a show of no hard feelings. Then all three were drifting across the street. Edie heard the good-natured ribbing start among them before they reached the other side.

'Are you all right?'

Will's question roused her from her stillness. Men, she thought, why do they think everything has to be settled by a fight?

'Who asked you to interfere?' she demanded because as far as she was concerned, she hadn't been in any danger at all. The resulting brawl had been completely unnecessary.

183

'No one. The boys were looking for some adventure. It's better that I supplied it instead of you,' he said, straightening a little and squaring his shoulders as if regathering his strength.

Her gaze narrowed in sharp suspicion as it occurred to her that he had not simply 'happened' to come this way. 'Why were you following me?'

'I realised that I hadn't told you how attractive your dress is with shoes.' His compliment reminded her of that afternoon when he had seen her trying the dress on barefoot, and some of her irritation faded with his remark. He lifted a hand to his cheek and wiped at it, and saw the glistening dark stain of blood on his fingers. 'One of those damned cowboys cut me with a ring,' he muttered under his breath.

'You'd better let me look at it.' She walked over to him and took the handkerchief he produced from a rear pocket. Folding it, she dabbed at the blood oozing from the gash on his cheekbone. In the shadowed night she couldn't tell the extent of the injury. 'There isn't enough light here.'

'There's a back entrance to this bar in the alley. The owner is a friend of mine. We can use his office in the rear.' With the first step he took towards the dark alley, he swayed unsteadily, and Edie was instantly at his side to curve an arm around his middle, offering him slim support. Will paused, leaning some of his weight on her until his legs were steady under him. He draped an arm across her shoulder, his hand closing on the soft flesh of her arm, and started into the alley. 'I haven't been in a fight for five years. If that third man had come at me I don't think I would have been standing at the end.'

'There wasn't any reason for that fight,' Edie remembered in a surge of impatience. 'They were letting me go when you showed up.'

'It didn't look that way to me.' The darkness of the alley enveloped them and Will made his way to the rear door by instinct alone. 'Either way, it's spilt milk now.' He rapped on the wooden door.

'As usual, a woman has to clean up the mess,' she murmured with the sharp edge of her tongue.

'As usual, she does.' His soft chuckle mocked her irritated response.

The door was opened by a portly, balding man in a tightly collared shirt with a string tie. His frowning glance widened to an open stare of shock as the interior light illuminated Will's face.

'It isn't as bad as it looks, Tubby,' Will assured the man in a dryly weary voice. But Edie felt the same start of shock at the smeared blood and purpling flesh around his cheekbone and jaw. She had taken care of too many of her children's cuts and bruises not to realise that his assessment was probably accurate.

'Come in, Will.' The owner opened the door wider to admit them. 'Sit here in my office and I'll go get a wet cloth and the first aid box.'

The stout man disappeared, exiting the private office through an interior door where the sounds of loud voices and a jukebox playing filtered into the room. Edie helped Will into a straight-backed chair beside the desk littered with papers, rolls of register tape, and delivery slips. Within seconds the owner returned with a clean wet cloth and the first aid kit. Edie took the cloth and knelt down to begin carefully wiping the blood smears from Will's face. The owner hovered beside her, gritting his teeth and making faces as if he was the patient.

'Do you think that cut will need stitches?' he asked. 'Maybe I should call a doctor?'

The wound had already stopped bleeding. Edie studied it carefully. 'It isn't as deep as it looks. I don't think it will need stitches,' she concluded, but she was well aware that a half an inch higher, and it would have been his eye that was cut. Her concern was overridden by irritation at his senseless risk that could have resulted in permanent injury. Her mouth thinned into a grimly angry line.

'Is there anything else I can do?' the owner offered. 'Anything you need?'

'I think we can manage alone,' Will replied. 'Thanks, Tubby.'

'I'll go out front and give Mike a hand at the bar. If you need me, just shout,' the man insisted.

'We will.' After the door latch had clicked shut, Will caught her eye with a glinting look. 'The poor guy can't stand the sight of blood.'

'It's a shame you don't suffer from the same problem. Maybe you wouldn't have ended up looking like this.' Her glance slashed over his face. There hadn't been as much damage as it had first appeared.

Except for the gash on his cheekbone, there was a bruise along his jaw and a purpling area near the cut. It could easily have been much worse.

Setting the stained wet cloth aside, Edie opened the first aid kit and removed a bottle of iodine. She used the applicator attached to the lid and dabbed some of the antiseptic into a corner of his wound. Will breathed in with a sharp, hissing sound and recoiled.

'Hold still,' she ordered without sympathy, and applied more iodine.

'Ouch!'

'I'd like to know what it is about iodine that can turn grown men into little boys—the same grown men who take fists in their face without a whimper,' she mocked him with a trace of acidity.

His grey eyes danced wickedly, not taking offence as they met her look. 'Maybe I'm missing the soothing hand on my brow.'

'You're getting just what you deserve.' She added an extra amount of iodine to what had already been applied.

'I was under the impression that a woman liked to have men fight over her,' he mocked.

'Not this woman,' Edie retorted. 'I don't think it ever occurred to you that someone could have been seriously hurt. You could have injured your eye, possibly lost the sight in it.' She re-capped the iodine bottle and straightened to return it to the first aid kit.

Will caught her wrist and turned her back to face him, his strong features tilted up to view her expression. His steady gaze seemed to penetrate behind her mask of irritation.

'I was beginning to think you didn't care,' he told her.

'It was stupid of you to fight.' She found it difficult to retain her lack of patience with him. 'You're too old for that sort of thing.'

'Too old?' He laughed heartily and pulled her on to his lap. 'I come to the aid of a damsel in distress and she accuses me of being *too old*!'

'I didn't mean it that way,' she protested. How could she when she was so fully aware of the powerful strength of his arms encircling her and his potently male vitality? The heat of his body was already stealing the force of her anger and kindling an entirely different response. 'I meant you

189

should have had more sense.'

'Where you're concerned, Edie, I seemed to have lost all ability to reason,' he said softly, and narrowed the distance between their lips until she felt the warmth of his breath against her skin. 'Hadn't you noticed?'

'No,' she whispered.

As his mouth settled on to her lips in a deep, searching kiss, her eyes closed and her arms found their way around his neck. In his arms, she found the fulfilment her heart had been seeking, and emotion swelled within her in a floodtide of intense longing.

His hand roamed over her stomach and ribs and burned through the soft fabric covering her breast. Tremors of desire quivered through her, caused by his caress. The driving pressure of his kiss told of his need, assuring her that she was not alone in this golden spiral of feelings.

There was a rough possession in the kisses he burned into her face and neck, claiming every inch of her. 'I'm not convinced any more that any man can arouse you like this, Edie,' he murmured thickly. 'You're showing me more than a purely sexual response.'

She rubbed her lips against his throat, savouring the taste of his skin. 'I'm not sure what I'm thinking or feeling.' With each drumming beat of her heart, she was becoming more sure of the love growing inside her for this man, but she kept it silent, betraying it only by deed but not by word.

Will sighed and reluctantly lifted his head. His grey eyes smouldered with barely disguised impatience and desire, yet his actions were controlled. He removed his hand from her breast and forced it to wander restlessly to her shoulder.

'Tubby will be coming back to see how we're doing,' he answered the question that was in her eyes. 'I think we should leave.'

'Yes,' she agreed, and let him help her off his lap. 'It's time I was going home.' She was disappointed when he failed to make an alternative suggestion.

'I'll walk you to your car,' was his only offer.

Edie waited by the back door while Will let the owner know they were leaving and thanked him for the help. He took her hand to lead her out of the alley to the lighted street and walked with her the half block to her car. He opened the driver's door for her and waited until she was behind the wheel to shut it.

'My car is parked around the corner,' he said. 'I'll follow you to make sure you get home in one piece.'

'Okay.' She smiled an instant agreement, glad that she hadn't seen the last of him this night.

Shortly after she pulled on to the highway, she saw the headlights of Will's car reflected in her rear-view mirror. It made her feel warm and wanted inside. All her adult life she had been the one who looked after others, and it was a novel experience to have someone looking after her. She rather liked the feeling.

The drive to the ranch didn't seem as long with his headlights winking in her mirror. There was a soft curve to her lips as she stopped the car in front of the house and climbed out. She waited for Will while he parked behind her car and stepped out.

'Would you like to come in for coffee?' she invited as he approached. 'It won't take long to fix some.'

'I was hoping you'd ask,' he replied, and took her arm as they climbed the porch steps to the front door.

Once inside, Edie paused to turn on a

light. 'Make yourself comfortable while I go in the kitchen and fix the coffee.'

She had already started in that direction when he called her name quietly yet insistently. 'Edie?'

She stopped and half-turned. 'Yes?'

He walked up to her and stopped. 'Coffee was just an excuse. We both know that.'

Her pulse accelerated its tempo and she suddenly had difficulty breathing. All conscious thought was swept aside by the dark intensity of his grey eyes, urgent and compelling. His hands curved on to the soft points of her shoulders, applying pressure to draw her towards him. The moment became protracted as he slowly bent his head and nuzzled the sensitive curve of her neck. A sigh of aching pleasure whispered from her lips.

She was absently amazed that someone so powerfully built could be so gentle yet firm. But Will seemed to be made from a series of contradictions. Here was a man strong enough to be gentle, ruthless enough to be kind, and arrogant enough to be vulnerable. His hands could easily crush her, yet he relied on the dominating influence of his demanding kisses to obtain her surrender. He didn't take, but persuaded her to give. He was a man hard enough to have a big heart.

'Edie, we've outgrown the stage of playing waiting games,' he murmured, and lifted his head to frame her face with his large hands. His callused skin was pleasantly abrasive, a rough caress. 'Leave that to Felicia and Jerry. We don't have any reason to play hard-to-get and those other games. It wastes too much precious time that we could be enjoying in other ways.'

'I'm not playing any games.' Her emotions were much too serious to be toyed with. She hoped he knew that.

'I want to make love to you, Edie.' The determination in his voice started a fluttering in the pit of her stomach. 'It's what you want, too. Don't try to deny it.'

'I won't, Will.' But she lowered her gaze to the leather stitching on his buckskin vest, feeling the tremors start.

'We've both been married. It isn't as if we don't know the score,' he insisted, and lowered his hands to the sides of her neck, his thumbs caressing her throat. A stillness came over him as he felt the faint tremors quaking through her body. 'You're trembling. What's wrong?'

194

'Nothing is wrong.' Not really. It was more a case of nerves than anything else. It certainly wasn't a lack of wanting on her part. 'It's just that I've never been to bed with any man other than my husband.'

'I know that.' He smiled into her uplifted gaze, but the puzzled light remained in his grey eyes.

'Don't you see?' The corners of her mouth deepened in a self-mocking smile. 'It would be like the first time all over again.'

A wondrous light flared in his eyes. 'My God, Edie!' he breathed, and gathered her into his arms, rubbing his neck against the softness of her hair. A shudder vibrated through his muscled frame. 'That's the most beautiful thing you could have said to me!'

'It isn't that I don't want you to love me, Will. It's just that I—' A pick-up rumbled into the ranchyard, and Edie drew back. 'It must be Jerry coming home.'

After taking a deep breath and releasing it, Will gave a wry shake of his head and let her go. Outside, a pair of truck doors slammed shut. 'And I thought it was only married couples who were interrupted by inquisitive children,' he murmured suggestively.

A smile was tugging at the corners of her mouth when Alison burst into the house. 'Mom, there's a strange car parked ... outside.' The last word was tacked belatedly on after she noticed Will standing near Edie. 'What are you doing here?' Surprise increased her natural bluntness.

'I was just making sure your mother arrived home safely,' Will replied, and exchanged a speaking glance with Edie.

'When I heard the truck,' Edie spoke up to divert the subject, 'I thought it was Jerry. I didn't expect to see you come through the door.'

'Oh, Jerry's home, too.' Alison glanced over her shoulder just as her half-brother entered the house. His glance stopped curiously on Will, too.

'You both came home together?' Edie looked at the two of them with faint surprise. 'But I thought—'

'It made more sense for me to ride with Rob as far as the Diamond D Ranch and come home from there with Jerry after he'd dropped Felicia off,' Alison explained the arrangement, then cocked her head to one side to study Will. 'What's happened to your face? It looks like you've been in a fight?'

He touched the iodine-coated gash on his cheekbone as if he had forgotten the wound. 'I fell down and cut myself,' he lied blandly.

'It must have been some fall,' Jerry observed sceptically. 'You cut one cheek and bruise the jaw on the other side.'

Edie knew they weren't going to be fooled by Will's story. 'There was a very minor incident tonight,' she admitted.

'What happened, Mom?' Alison moved quickly to her side and Jerry followed.

Will answered the question. 'Some young men were getting fresh with your mother, and I merely reminded them of their manners.' His glance ran over the three of them, standing together side by side. Wry amusement flickered across his features. 'The Three Musketeers are united again,' he drawled.

'One for all and all for one,' Alison returned brightly.

'I'm having a few friends over for a barbecue tomorrow. I'd like you to come.' He looked at Edie as he offered the invitation, but his gaze quickly encompassed the three of them. 'All of you.'

Edie was aware of the shocked silence emanating from her daughter and stepson, but she felt absolutely no hesitation about accepting his invitation. So much had changed in the space of one evening. She simply couldn't regard Maddock as an enemy any longer.

'Thank you, Maddock. It sounds fun,' she smiled under the intimate look in those grey eyes.

'Come early—around eleven-thirty. I want to show you around my home.' The softness of his voice carried its own message.

Typically he left without a goodbye, but Edie discovered she was becoming used to that. With his departure, Jerry and Alison finally had a chance to voice their curiosity. Jerry was first.

'What's going on, Edie?' he frowned.

'Yes,' Alison echoed his question, 'why do we suddenly rate an invitation to Sunday dinner?'

Edie had a lot of guesses of her own, but she only voiced the safest one. 'Maybe he's finally decided that we're here to stay.'

CHAPTER TEN

The Diamond D ranch house was a white, two-storeyed building with a pillared front. It faced the ranch buildings and had a spectacular view of the rough and broken Dakota terrain. This was Edie's first glimpse of the ranch headquarters, and she stared openly at its structures and network of corrals.

By the time Jerry had parked the car in front of the house, Will was outside to greet them. 'Welcome to the Diamond D.' He reserved a warm look for Edie. 'I'm sorry Felicia isn't on hand to greet you, but she's still upstairs getting ready. Come inside.'

His hand rested in light possession on the back of her waist as he personally escorted her to the front door with Jerry and Alison trailing behind them. The foyered entrance to the house included a staircase to the second floor. To the right, decorated in soft rusts and golds, was the living room where Will began his tour of the house. A fireplace built of native stone gave the room a relaxed, comfortable air.

'There are three fireplaces in the house,

two downstairs and one upstairs,' he explained as he led them into the dining room.

There was an informal quality about the room. It was easy for Edie to imagine Will sitting at the head of a tableful of guests, discussing the ranch or politics or something as basic as Johnny's first tooth. Despite the richness of the solid walnut table, chairs and sideboard, there was something essentially casual about the room.

A cook was busy in the kitchen with preparations for the noon barbecue, so they didn't linger long there. But Edie did notice that it was equipped with all the latest conveniences with plenty of work space and a breakfast nook.

The last room he showed them on the ground floor was the den, panelled in knotty pine with leather-upholstered furniture. The bookshelves were lined with volumes on animal husbandry and agriculture interspersed with a selection of fiction novels. Issues of ranch-related magazines were scattered about the room, giving it a lived-in look. The second fireplace was located in the den, constructed of burnt brick.

As they returned to the foyer, Edie realised this was definitely a rancher's house where a man could feel free to walk in straight from the ranchyard without worrying greatly about what he tracked on to the floors. He could bring in a new-born calf, half frozen by a winter's storm, and let the warmth of the kitchen nurse it back to life. Despite its imposing size, it was a home.

'We'll have the barbecue on the patio in the backyard by the pool.' He paused beside the thermo-paned glass doors that opened from the foyer on to the patio. 'Last night I forgot to suggest that you bring your swimming suits along, but there's a small selection of styles and sizes in the changing room that we keep on hand for guests.'

'Look!' Alison pointed to an object out of Edie's sight. 'There's Rob.'

'Yes,' Will affirmed her statement. 'He's helping set up the tables.'

'Let's give him a hand, Jerry.' Alison was quick to find a reason to see him again.

'Go ahead,' Will nodded when Jerry hesitated to agree with his half-sister's suggestion. 'We'll be out shortly.' As the two slid open the glass doors, the hand on Edie's back applied pressure to steer her

201

away from the doors, and Will wandered, apparently aimlessly, to the centre of the foyer. 'That concludes the tour of the house, with the exception of the upstairs,' he corrected with a glance at the staircase. 'There are five bedrooms in all, counting the master suite.' He turned her round to face him, resting his hands on her hips. 'What do you think of it?'

'Between the house and the ranch buildings, I'm convinced we'll never be able to approach your scale of operation,' Edie admitted. 'If your intention was to impress me, you've succeeded.'

His mouth thinned with displeasure. Her reply wasn't the one he wanted to hear. 'I'm not interested in impressing you. I want to know what you think of my home. Is it someplace you'd like to live? Do you like it?'

'I like it, yes.' Edie hesitated to say more, certain she was reading more into his question than he intended.

'That's why I wanted you to come today—so you could see where I live and get to know my friends. It probably seems like I'm rushing things—and I am,' he admitted with a flash of wry amusement. 'But I know what I want, Edie. I want to

202

marry you. I want you to be my wife.'

'Will!' Amazement, a wondrous kind of disbelief, and a little shock became all mixed up in the issuance of his name. She hadn't expected a proposal, but she knew the answer she wanted to give him, only the words wouldn't come out.

He gazed into her eyes, shining with happiness, and read his answer. A slow smile of satisfaction curved his firmly cut mouth. His head started to bend towards her, and stopped when he heard car doors slam outside and voices signalling the approach of guests.

Before the arriving guests reached the front door, he claimed her lips in a hard, possessive kiss that revealed his desire and frustration. She clung to his kiss for an instant, then let him draw away.

'We'll talk about this later—after everyone has left,' he told her as someone knocked on the door. But the light in his grey eyes promised there would be less talking and more action.

When he left her to welcome his guests at the door, Edie was lost in a bliss-filled daze. A faint noise came from the stairs and she turned. Felicia Maddock stood poised on the steps halfway down. It became quickly evident to Edie that the girl had been there for some time. She saw the cold hurt of jealousy in Felicia's blue eyes as they bored into her. Ignoring her father at the door with the arriving friends, Felicia came swinging down the steps directly towards Edie, her expression coldly haughty.

'I knew Daddy wanted your ranch,' Felicia announced. 'But it never occurred to me that he wanted it badly enough to marry *you* to get it.'

With her poisoned barb delivered, Felicia swept past, not allowing Edie a chance to reply. In numbed shock, she watched the girl walk to Will's side to gaily welcome their guests. Was it possible that the motive behind Will's proposal was to obtain control of the ranch?

When he called her forward to introduce her to his friends, Edie knew it wasn't true. Will Maddock fought for what he wanted, and fought hard, but he wasn't the kind to resort to underhanded tactics. He was too blunt, too forthright.

No, Felicia had deliberately implanted that seed of doubt hoping it would germinate and grow, nourished by Edie's fertile imagination. The ranch had always been a wedge between Edie and Will, and

Felicia wanted to keep it that way. But she'd made a mistake, because Edie knew Will too well to believe that about him.

He kept Edie at his side as he led his party of guests outside to the patio. She managed to take an absent part in the conversation swirling around her and answer questions put to her by his friends, but her thoughts kept running back to Felicia.

Halfway through the meal of barbecued ribs and chicken, it occurred to Edie why Felicia had made such a vicious remark. It had been jealousy she had seen in the girl's expression. For years she had been the only female in her father's life, spoiled and pampered and indulged by him. She was the mistress of the house.

If Will married Edie, all that would change. Felicia felt threatened. Edie would not only usurp her position as lady of the house, but she would also become the object of her father's affection and attention. And, childlike, Felicia didn't want to share him. She resented Edie, just as she would resent any woman she felt might come between her and her father.

The situation troubled Edie. Knowing the problem did not automatically provide a solution. There had to be a way to handle it if she had just time to think, but that was impossible with so many people around.

After everyone had finished their meal, there was a general disinclination to move from the tables. When Edie noticed Felicia at the buffet table replenishing her iced tea, she saw an opportunity to speak to the girl.

'I'm going to get some more iced tea,' she murmured her excuse to Will, and rose from the table. She crossed the patio to the end of the buffet where the insulated urn of iced tea was located. When Felicia saw her approach, she started to walk away. 'Felicia,' Edie called out quickly to stop the girl, 'I'd like to speak to you a moment.'

'I can't think of a thing that we would possibly have to say to one another,' the girl replied with obvious disdain.

'There's something we need to get straightened out,' Edie insisted quietly but firmly. 'I think you've misunderstood some things.'

'No, you're the one who doesn't understand,' Felicia retorted. Edie saw Jerry and Alison approaching the buffet table, but Felicia's back was to them and she was unaware there was anyone within hearing except Edie. 'Daddy and I have tried to make it clear to you from the beginning. You aren't wanted here. You never have been. Regardless of what you might think now, that hasn't changed.'

'Felicia—' Edie tried to warn the girl that Alison and Jerry were listening. Anger had already turned Jerry's mouth grim and brought the fighting sparks to Alison's eyes.

'You wanted to talk,' the girl reminded her that the conversation had been Edie's idea. 'So you might as well listen to some advice. You've had your free meal, so why don't you leave?'

'I think that's an excellent idea, Mother,' Alison spoke up, and Felicia pivoted in surprise. 'I know when I'm not wanted.'

'Jerry!' Felicia gasped in dismay.

'I always knew you were a spoiled, selfish brat,' he said tightly. 'You've grown way too big for your britches.'

Before anyone could guess his intention, Jerry scooped Felicia off her feet and into his arms. She shrieked in alarm, but didn't struggle too hard to get free. Edie sank her teeth into her lower lip as she realised that everyone at the barbecue was watching them, including Will, who had stood up.

'Jerry, put me down!' Felicia protested,

but he continued to walk, carrying her in his arms. 'What *are* you doing?'

Edie had already guessed when she noticed that he was walking towards the swimming pool. An instant later, Felicia reached the same conclusion. She screamed something about him ruining her dress, but it was too late. He was at the edge of the pool and heaving her into the water. Jerry waited long enough to see her splutter to the surface, then turned to rejoin Edie and Alison.

'I think we'd better leave,' he said to Edie above the confused laughter and the rush of people to the pool to help Felicia out of the water. Will was among them.

Under the circumstances, Edie felt leaving was the wisest choice. 'Yes, I think we should.' Explanations would have to be made to Will, but it could be done later. This was not the time.

'I wish I had a picture of that,' Alison murmured as they entered the house through the sliding doors. 'Only you could do that and get by with it, Jerry.'

'She needed to be turned upside down and spanked,' he muttered.

'I feel sorry for her. She's so confused and insecure,' Edie sighed, and glanced at the staircase rising from the foyer.

'Felicia?' Alison gave her a wide look. 'Are you sure we're talking about the same girl?'

'Yes, I—' Edie wasn't able to finish her explanation as the sliding glass doors to the patio opened behind them. All three glanced back when they heard it.

Will came striding across the entry hall. 'Where the hell do you think you're going?' The low demand was taut and angry, the hard steel of his gaze directed at Edie.

Alison and Jerry immediately closed ranks around her, showing a united front. 'Under the circumstances, Will, we thought it was best to leave,' Edie explained.

'I suggest you change your mind,' he ordered tersely. 'You're staying here.'

'We don't take orders,' Alison retorted. 'Certainly not from you!'

'Edie had nothing to do with what happened by the pool,' stated Jerry, moving forward to take the brunt of Will's anger. 'I was the one who threw Felicia in the water. And I'm not going to apologise for it either. She deserved worse than that for the things she said to Edie.'

Will's stone-grey eyes flicked over Jerry

and Alison with hard impatience. 'This is a private discussion between Edie and myself. You have no business interfering in it.'

'Will—' Edie bristled at his censuring tone as the air crackled with tension.

'Be quiet, Edie,' he snapped. 'I'm going to get this straightened out once and for all. There'll be plenty of times in the future when I'll be raising my voice at you over something. There isn't any way that every time we argue, I'm going to take on the whole Gibbs family. It's time they learned to keep out of any discussion between a man and his wife!'

'His wife?' Alison frowned and glanced at Edie. 'What's he talking about, Mom?'

'This isn't the way I wanted you to find out,' Edie said, and flashed an irritated glance at Will. Everything had mushroomed out of control. 'He asked me to marry him.' Just saying the words seemed to make it more real. In spite of her defensive anger, her voice softened as she made the announcement.

'Are you?' was Alison's instant and slightly incredulous reaction.

But Jerry had been watching her expression and noticed the way her gaze had sought Will when she told them. He guessed what her answer had been and bent his head to kiss her cheek. 'Dad would be happy for you, Edie,' he said to ease her mind. 'I'm glad you found somebody else, too.' He smiled, then turned to Will and offered his hand. 'Congratulations. You've got yourself quite a woman.'

'Yes, I know.' Will's roughly hewn features were gentled by the warmth of his look as he held Edie's gaze. The possessive light burning in his grey eyes started a tingling in her nerve ends.

For Alison, none of it had truly sunk in. She glanced around in helpless confusion. 'I don't understand,' she murmured.

'I'll explain it to her,' Jerry smiled at Edic and took his sistcr by thc hand to lcad her away so Edie could be alone with Will. 'It's this way, Alison,' he began as they walked away. 'There's this emotion called "love".'

Edie didn't hear any more than that as his voice trailed away. Will had taken a step towards her, his large hands settling on to her shoulders while his gaze searched her face.

'Don't ever walk away like that again, Edie.' This time it was a request. 'Why did you do it? You know I asked you to stay until the others had left.'

'Yes,' she admitted, her voice growing soft. 'But, after that incident with Felicia—'

'What on earth did she say to you?' An amused frown flickered across his forehead. 'It was all I could do to keep from laughing when Jerry dumped her in the pool.'

'It doesn't really matter what she said,' Edie insisted.

'Yes, it does if it was something against you,' he corrected firmly.

She realised it would all come out sooner or later. 'She doesn't want you to marry me.'

'I know.' There was a wry twist to his mouth. 'When I told her this morning, she threw a tantrum. That's why she was upstairs sulking when you arrived.'

'She tried to convince me that the only reason you wanted to marry me was to get the ranch,' Edie admitted.

His hands tightened on her shoulders as his gaze became piercing. 'You didn't believe that? Is that why you were leaving?'

'No.' She smiled and shook her head. 'You may want our ranch, but I don't think you would go to the extreme of marrying me just to get your hands on it. It wouldn't

212

work anyway.'

'I never for a minute thought it would.' His look gentled. 'I'm sure that you plan to turn the ranch over to Jerry and Alison after we're married. But I still don't think any of you realise the mammoth job you're tackling before the ranch will show a profit.'

'There's something you haven't known about us.' Her eyes danced with the one fact they had kept from him. 'Joe left us an income independent of the ranch. We weren't gambling all of our money.'

'I should have known,' Will chuckled. 'I think I stopped caring about getting the ranch when you outsmarted me and bought those cattle in Wyoming. That's just about the time I started falling in love with you, too.'

She caught her breath, a sudden radiance shining in her expression. 'Do you realise that is the first time you've told me that, Will Maddock?'

'Told you what? That I love you?' His gaze roamed over her face. 'I thought I'd been telling you that every time I looked at you.'

'You have,' she said softly. 'But it's nice to hear the actual words.'

213

An encircling arm pulled her against his rugged frame while his large hand became tangled in her hair. She melted against him, her lips parting as his mouth moved over them in clear possession. Joy sang through her veins, pure and sweet, a pleasure so strong that she hadn't believed it could exist. The depth of her love for him left her breathless. Her hands were spread across his broad back, feeling the tautly rigid muscles.

Will finally called a halt to the kiss before it went out of control. His breathing was as heavy as her own as he lifted his head, and raw desire smouldered in the look that scanned her love-soft features.

'We're going to be married next week, Edie,' he told her. 'If I could arrange it, it would be this afternoon.'

'But what about Felicia?' She gently reminded him of his daughter's disapproval. 'Maybe we should give her time to get used to the idea.'

'Time isn't going to help her—and it would be hell for me,' he declared with a wicked glint in his eyes. 'I haven't done a very good job of raising my daughter. She needs you as much as I do . . . well, almost as much as I do,' he qualified that.

214

'It isn't going to be easy for her,' Edie warned, and caressed his hard cheek. 'She's used to being the only woman in your life.'

'I think Jerry can handle that problem.' The corners of his mouth deepened with a smile. 'I have the feeling that ranch is going to wind up in the Maddock family yet.'

'You're incorrigible!' she laughed.

'No, I'm in love. And that can be contagious,' he replied.

'It certainly can,' she agreed, and lifted her lips to receive his.

The publishers hope that this
Large Print Book has brought
you pleasurable reading.
Each title is designed to make
the text as easy to see as possible.
G. K. Hall Large Print Books are
available from your library and
your local bookstore. Or you can
receive information on upcoming
and current Large Print Books by
mail and order directly from the
publisher. Just send your name
and address to:

G. K. Hall & Co.
70 Lincoln Street
Boston, Mass. 02111

or call, toll-free:

1–800–343–2806